~ HIS VIRGIN MISTRESS ~

THE SHEIKH'S VIRGIN PRINCESS

SARAH MORGAN

Bedded by command!

HARLEQUIN Presents

EXTRA

HIS VIRGIN MISTRESS
Bedded by command!

He's wealthy and commanding, with the
self-assurance of a man who knows he has power.
He's used to sophisticated, confident women who
fit easily into his glamorous world.

She's an innocent virgin, inexperienced and awkward,
yet eager to find a man worthy of her love.

Sweeping her off her feet and into his bed,
he'll show her the most exquisite pleasure,
and demand she be his mistress!

ISBN-13:978-0-373-52701-4
ISBN-10: 0-373-52701-2

S EAN

**Don't miss any of the
fabulous stories this month
from Presents EXTRA!**

HPEATMIFC0109

Confronted by her first ever vision of a naked man, Alexa fixed her eyes on this impromptu display of rampant masculinity, and only when she heard his sharply indrawn breath did she finally manage to drag her eyes upward.

But instead of respite, she was offered just another angle on impressive manhood. Wide, powerful shoulders, curving muscles honed by hard physical exercise, and a broad, strong chest hazed by curling, dark hairs.

No wonder she hadn't been able to resist his kiss.

"The blushing is sweet, but a little over the top given the kiss we just shared." Karim's tone was icy cold as he reached for the robe that was flung carelessly over the chair. Without any obvious sign of haste, he slid his arms into the sleeves and belted it loosely, as relaxed and cool as she was embarrassed. "And your display of shyness is a little out of place in a woman who began exploring her sexuality at such a young age. But if you want to play that game then I'm happy to oblige. It's safe to look, Your Highness."

Safe?

SARAH MORGAN was born in Wiltshire and started writing at the age of eight, when she produced an autobiography of her hamster.

At the age of eighteen, she traveled to London to train as a nurse in one of London's top teaching hospitals, and she describes those years as extremely happy and definitely censored!

She worked in a number of areas after she qualified, but her favorite was the accident and emergency department, where she found the work stimulating and fun. Nowhere else in the hospital environment did she encounter such good teamwork between doctors and nurses.

By now her interests had moved on from hamsters to men, and she started writing romance fiction.

Her first completed manuscript, written after the birth of her first child, was rejected but the comments were encouraging, so she tried again. On the third attempt, her manuscript *Worth the Risk* was accepted unchanged. She describes receiving the acceptance letter as one of the best moments of her life, after meeting her husband and having her two children.

Sarah still works part-time in a health-related industry and spends the rest of the time with her family, trying to squeeze in writing whenever she can. She is an enthusiastic skier and walker, and loves outdoor life.

THE SHEIKH'S
VIRGIN PRINCESS
SARAH MORGAN

~ HIS VIRGIN MISTRESS ~

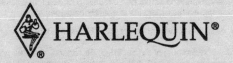

HARLEQUIN®

TORONTO • NEW YORK • LONDON
AMSTERDAM • PARIS • SYDNEY • HAMBURG
STOCKHOLM • ATHENS • TOKYO • MILAN • MADRID
PRAGUE • WARSAW • BUDAPEST • AUCKLAND

Recycling programs
for this product may
not exist in your area.

ISBN-13: 978-0-373-52701-4
ISBN-10:   0-373-52701-2

THE SHEIKH'S VIRGIN PRINCESS

First North American Publication 2009.

Copyright © 2007 by Sarah Morgan.

www.eHarlequin.com

Printed in U.S.A.

THE SHEIKH'S
VIRGIN PRINCESS

PROLOGUE

'FIND me a way out of this. *And find it fast!*' Simmering with rage and frustration, the Sultan paced across the thick Persian carpet, and then turned and glared at the group of men who sat in frozen silence around the polished, antique table. 'Time is running out, and I tell you now that I *will not marry that woman!*'

His announcement was met by a collective gasp of dismay, and his team of advisors conferred hastily, their communication a series of babbled suggestions and nervous gestures unlikely to produce a satisfactory solution to any problem, let alone one of huge national importance.

They are like stunned rabbits, the Sultan thought grimly as he viewed them with mounting exasperation.

'Your Excellency.' One of the lawyers rose to his feet, his hands shaking. 'We have looked through all the past statutes. There is no way out of this marriage.'

'Then look again.' His voice deadly soft, the Sultan watched as the man paled. 'Look again and find *something* we can use— something that allows us to break this ridiculous contract.'

'That's the problem, Your Excellency.' The lawyer's fingers gripped the edge of the table that provided the only barrier between him and the Sultan. 'There isn't anything. There is no precedent for this. Your father made this agreement with the late Crown

Prince of Rovina sixteen years ago, a few months before his un-
timely death. They were at school together, and in the army—'

'I don't need a lecture on *why* I find myself in this situation,'
the Sultan growled. 'Just advice on how to extricate myself. Fast.'

'There is no way out, Your Excellency. You have to marry the
Princess Alexandra of Rovina.' As he delivered the final blow,
the lawyer's voice shook. 'Perhaps she will be an asset…' he ventured timidly, his words tailing off as he met the Sultan's hard,
cynical stare.

'You think so? "The rebel princess"—isn't that what they
call my wife-to-be? Since she was old enough to attend school,
this girl has left a trail of chaos behind her. She drives her cars
too fast, parties until she is unconscious and treats sex as if it were
an Olympic sport. And she's not even twenty-four years old.
Please enlighten me as to how such a woman could possibly be
an asset to Zangrar.'

A deathly silence followed his question, and the Sultan raised
an eyebrow. 'Nothing comes to mind?' Their lack of response
frustrated him to the point of explosion, and he turned and walked
towards the window, struggling with his temper and *hating* himself for that loss of control. 'Leave me. All of you. Leave!'

There was an undignified scrambling, and the room emptied
in a matter of moments in response to his abrupt order.

As the door closed behind them, the Sultan rubbed his long
fingers over his forehead, trying to ease the ache and access
rational thought. He didn't know which sickened him more: *the
thought of marriage generally, or the thought of marriage to a
woman like the Princess Alexandra.* By all accounts she was a
woman who appeared to possess all those traits that had made
him renounce the institution of marriage at a young age. She was
shallow, brainless and a princess only by an unfortunate accident
of birth. There was nothing royal about her behaviour, and there
was no way she was going to become his wife.

She was exactly the sort of woman who would have caught the attention of his father.

A sound came from behind him, and he turned swiftly, his eyes narrowing as he saw his chief advisor standing behind him. 'Omar?'

'Your Excellency.' The man stepped forward. 'If I might be permitted to venture a suggestion…'

'If this suggestion involves marriage, please save your breath.'

'It is understandable that Your Excellency would have strong feelings on the subject, given your late father's somewhat unfortunate history.'

The Sultan felt every muscle in his body tense. 'That is *not* a subject I wish to discuss.'

'Indeed, Your Excellency, and yet it is germane to the current situation. You are right to be concerned. The people of Zangrar will not tolerate another woman like your stepmother.'

The Sultan inhaled slowly. 'You are unusually brave in your choice of conversation topic, Omar. You may have known me since I was two years old, but don't presume too far. I'm experiencing some difficulties with anger management.'

Omar gave a faint smile. 'In the circumstances your anger is understandable. What you have achieved for Zangrar since your father's death is nothing short of amazing. You have given hope to every citizen, and now you are afraid that you will lose what has been gained.'

'And that is what will happen if I marry this woman.'

'Possibly. But Your Excellency *does* need a wife, that fact is not in dispute,' Omar murmured. 'Your people are anxious for you to fall in love and wed.'

The Sultan suppressed an unexpected desire to laugh out loud. 'I am prepared to make many personal sacrifices for the good of my country, but falling in love will not be one of them. In time, I will choose a wife who can give me children. But she will not be some wild, untamed European princess. The people of Zangrar deserve better.'

Omar cleared his throat delicately. 'But the Princess Alexandra *is* of royal blood. In one year from now, on her twenty-fifth birthday, her uncle the regent steps down and she ascends the throne of Rovina.'

'Meaning that she will be in a position to bring even greater chaos to her country?'

Omar allowed himself a smile. 'Meaning that an alliance between our two countries would offer many increased opportunities that would benefit Zangrar. Trade, tourism—'

'Am I supposed to overlook her embarrassing reputation and overall lack of dignity?'

'The Princess Alexandra is said to be quite astonishingly beautiful. Given your own success with women, the simplest approach might be for Your Excellency simply to urge her to moderate her behaviour. It is no secret that you enjoy the company of beautiful women.'

'In a *wife* I place moral stature above any physical attributes,' the Sultan growled, feeling his frustration mount. 'However, my views on the subject are apparently not relevant, since it appears that there is no way I can break this ridiculous contract my father made.' Of the legacy of stupidity and weakness left by his father, this was the issue that angered him most, because it threatened everything he had worked for.

Omar's expression was thoughtful. 'That is true, Your Excellency. There is no way *you* can break the contract.'

Something in his tone made the Sultan narrow his eyes. 'Omar?'

His chief advisor smiled placidly. 'I have studied the contract in minute detail, and it is true that there is no way for you to break the agreement that your father made.' He paused. 'But *she* can.'

The Sultan straightened his powerful shoulders. 'You're saying that the princess has the right to veto this marriage?'

'Absolutely. But, before Your Excellency becomes unduly encouraged by that option, I should tell you that there has been no hint of dissent from the principality of Rovina. It would appear that the princess is eager to marry you.'

'And we both know why.' His mouth set in a grim line, the Sultan contemplated everything he'd read about the Princess Alexandra. 'Rovina's coffers are empty, and her spending powers are as legendary as her rebel behaviour.'

'That could be part of it, but maybe not all. Your Excellency is extremely handsome. You are considered to be something of a matrimonial prize.'

The Sultan gave a humourless laugh and then paced over to the window, his expression bleak. A prize? If the princess knew what she would be taking on, then she wouldn't be so eager to proceed with the wedding. *As cold as the desert at night*—wasn't that how the last female in his life had bitterly described him when he'd abruptly ended the relationship?

He stared down into the courtyard below, wondering why that description didn't bother him more. Possibly because it was true. *He wasn't capable of love*; he knew that. But nor did he see that as a reason for regret. He'd seen what love could do to a person, and he wasn't interested in sacrificing his judgement in exchange for emotional anguish. What *did* interest him was acting responsibly for the good of his country. And marrying the most notorious princess in Europe wasn't going to achieve that objective.

He turned to Omar, his movements swift and decisive. 'You are sure that the princess has the right to break this contract?'

'Absolutely. The only person who can free you from this wedding is the woman herself.'

'Then it will be done.' The Sultan gave a satisfied nod. 'Omar, you have excelled yourself.'

'Your Excellency, I hardly need to remind you that the princess *does* want to marry you, so the details of the contract are somewhat irrelevant.'

'*Not* irrelevant,' the Sultan drawled softly. 'The princess may wish to marry me at the moment, but given time and a little— *persuasion*—I'm confident that she will soon see that this marriage is not for her.'

'You plan to influence her decision, Your Excellency?'

'Absolutely. The problem is solved, Omar. The Princess Alexandra is going to decide that marriage to me would be an *extremely* bad idea. And, given that most women are appallingly indecisive, we are going to offer her every assistance in reaching that conclusion. I intend to see to it personally.' He gave a grim smile.

No matter what she had in mind, she would *not* be marrying the Sultan.

CHAPTER ONE

THE blades of the swords clashed viciously, and the room rang with the sharp sound of metal on metal.

Karim tightened his hand on the hilt of the sabre and lunged, sending his blade towards his opponent's torso with a burst of explosive power that drew a collective gasp from the observers gathered around the room.

Karim ignored them. All his attention was focused on his opponent, whose identity was concealed by the dark mesh of the protective fencing-mask.

Attack, counter attack. Lunge, feint, parry.

They fought with relentless aggression, each trying to out-manoeuvre the other as they fenced for supremacy. The referee stood frozen to the spot, silenced by the sheer ferocity of the duel taking place in front of him.

Even as he fought, Karim was studying his opponent, trying to anticipate his moves. And failing. For the first time in his life, he was equally matched. His nameless, faceless opponent was changing his strategy for each attack, his movements swift and skilled, his footwork immaculate. The man was slight of build, but he moved with the speed and agility of a true athlete.

Karim felt the sweat prickle between his shoulder blades as the pace and intensity of the fight increased.

When he'd been informed that the Princess Alexandra had insisted on watching him fence before agreeing to let him be her bodyguard for the journey to Zangrar, he'd been both amused and irritated. Clearly, she was a real prima donna. It was the first time he'd fought in response to a feminine whim, and he'd strolled into the room prepared to thrash his opponent in a matter of minutes. Instead he was being seriously challenged in a sport at which he'd considered himself unbeatable.

Unaccustomed to meeting anyone who had either the nerve or the skill to take him on, Karim had been pleasantly surprised to discover that his anonymous opponent possessed both qualities in abundance, along with technical and tactical depth. He was even more astonished to discover that he was enjoying himself.

Who was the man in the mask?

Protocol demanded that fencing opponents salute each other at the start of each bout, and his opponent had observed that protocol, but he'd also entered the room fully prepared, his mask already in place.

Accustomed to boredom, Karim felt the adrenaline surge inside him, and vowed to reveal the identity of his partner. Whoever it was would be fencing him again, he vowed as he parried and then thrust, his movements confident and aggressive. The blade struck home in a lightning-fast attack, the force of the blow absorbed by the flex of the blade.

His opponent stepped backwards, his body already poised for the next attack, and Karim gave a low laugh of admiration. Although the man was slightly lacking in height, he was bold and fearless, attacking with an energy and confidence that was unusual.

Briefly distracted by girlish laughter, Karim cast a swift, irritated glance towards the spectators, his attention momentarily drawn to a group of women watching with flirtatious interest.

Which one of those was the Princess Alexandra?

And what indulgent, feminine whim had driven her to demand that he prove himself in this fight before allowing him the honour of becoming her bodyguard? Obviously she was spoiled, bored and entertained by the idea of men fighting for her. *Did she enjoy blood sports?*

He turned his attention back to his adversary, anger giving speed to his attack, but his opponent parried with a renewed burst of energy, grimly determined not to yield a single point.

Karim was as intrigued as he was challenged.

If he hadn't known better, he would have thought that the duel was personal.

And yet how could it be personal when they didn't even know each other?

Deciding that the match had gone on long enough, Karim made the most of his superior strength and speed and executed a perfect lunge that won him the final point.

Breathing heavily, he dragged off his mask.

'My match.' He held out his hand as protocol dictated. 'So, having slain the dragon, I presume I've now won the right to protect the princess. Perhaps you would introduce me so that I can be given my next challenge? Pistols at dawn, perhaps? Remove your mask. I deserve to see the face of the man I just fought.'

His opponent hesitated, and then dragged off the mask. '*Not a man.*' She spoke in a warm, husky voice designed by mother nature to bring the entire opposite sex to its knees, and Karim inhaled sharply as a mass of golden, coppery hair tumbled over narrow shoulders. Even though he knew the dangers that often lurked behind extreme physical beauty, he was blinded.

Observing his reaction with wry amusement, she held out a slender hand and spoke again. This time her voice was soft, as if she were afraid of being overheard. 'I'm Princess Alexandra. And you're supposed to be my bodyguard. The problem is, I don't actually *want* a bodyguard. You weren't supposed to win the match. I'm afraid you've had a wasted journey.'

She'd lost!

Desperately hoping that he couldn't see how much her legs were shaking, Alexa watched incredulity flicker across his handsome face as he acknowledged her identity. And he *was* handsome, she conceded as she brushed her damp hair away from her flushed cheeks. Handsome and strong.

She'd felt the power in his body as he'd fought with what could only be described as restrained masculine aggression. And she sensed that he'd been far from reaching the limits of his capabilities. His broad shoulders and muscular physique suggested that fencing was only one of many activities that he enjoyed in his pursuit of a physical challenge.

She should have picked a different sport.

And now he was watching her intently, his dark gaze arrogant and assured as he slowly loosened the fastening at the neck of his jacket to reveal a tantalizing hint of bronzed skin, shiny with the sweat of physical exertion. His eyes demanded that she look only at him, as if he were determined to read everything about her in one searing glance.

Trapped by the force of his bold gaze, Alexa felt something dangerous and unfamiliar flicker to life, and then a hot, instantaneous explosion of sexual awareness engulfed her. Her body burned and melted, and the feeling was deeply shocking because, although she was accustomed to being on the receiving end of male attention, she was *not* accustomed to responding.

Her knees weakened by the fire in her pelvis, she nevertheless forced herself to hold his gaze, waiting for him to back down and display the deference and respect that she knew was due to her.

He was a bodyguard.

She was a royal princess. Despite her less-than-enviable position in the royal household, she was accustomed to being greeted with the appropriate formality by strangers, but this man clearly wasn't daunted or in any way impressed by her title or position. Instead he held himself tall and proud, his posture one of authority and command, as if he was used to giving orders and being instantly obeyed.

Clearly, he was someone *extremely* senior in the Sultan's security team, Alexa mused as her eyes trailed from his almost-perfect bone structure to the firm, sensual curve of his mouth. *Powerful,* she thought. If she had to find one word to describe the man in front of her, then it would be *powerful,* and she felt her stomach lurch. When the Sultan had promised a bodyguard to escort her on the journey, she'd expected someone who would follow orders.

This man didn't look as though he'd ever followed an order in his life.

Which made the situation extremely awkward. She didn't want him as her bodyguard. She didn't trust him. She didn't trust *anyone.* Whatever happened, she had to be in charge of her own safety; it was the only way she would ever escape from the tangled mess of her life.

She couldn't believe that this moment had arrived—*that she'd actually survived this far.* Her brain fluttered around the edges of panic, as it always did when she considered her impending marriage to the Sultan of Zangrar.

It wasn't that she was afraid of him. She wasn't. Having lived the life she'd lived for the past sixteen years, she no longer cared that he was reputed to be ruthless, controlling and totally devoid of emotion. In a way, it actually helped, knowing that he didn't have a sensitive side, because she didn't have to feel guilty about forcing him into a marriage that was so lacking in romance.

There was no escaping from the fact that, in normal circumstances, this marriage would be the last thing she wanted. But her circumstances weren't normal, and this marriage wasn't about what was best for *her*; it was about what was best for Rovina.

Her hand tightened on the hilt of the sabre. She'd reviewed her options so many times that her brain felt raw with thinking, and no matter how often she circled round the issue she always ended up at the same place.

The future of Rovina depended on her marriage to the Sultan.

And now that goal was *finally* within reach.

Only a journey now stood between her and Zangrar.

But it would be a hazardous journey, and she would need to have her wits about her. Ironic though it seemed, the *last* thing she wanted was a bodyguard. Having him there would simply put her life at greater risk.

A giggle from the women watching reminded her that they were becoming the subject of scrutiny and gossip, and Alexa smiled, reminding herself that she had an image to keep up: *the image of a woman with nothing more serious on her mind except the pursuit of frivolous pleasures.*

'You can go home, bodyguard.' She removed the glove from her fencing hand and spoke softly so that only he could hear. 'I don't need your protection.' Her words provoked a sharp intake of breath from the man standing in front of her.

'My protection is *not* optional.' His dark eyes glinted dangerously as he studied her face. 'You and I need to speak alone. Now.'

Startled by his autocratic tone, Alexa opened her mouth to refuse, but he closed long, strong fingers around her wrist and propelled her bodily towards the ante-room where the fencing equipment was stored, apparently indifferent to the curious stares of those watching.

He'd been fighting a woman?

Tension erupting inside him, Karim released her and slammed

the door to the ante-room shut with the flat of his hand, his eyes fixed on the cascading mass of soft, silky curls that poured down her back. *Her hair was the colour of a desert sunset.* And that first glance into her eyes had been like throwing himself onto a burning spear. His body had been consumed by the most basic of sexual urges, the chemistry between them so hot and instantaneous that for a moment he'd been able to think only of sex.

'Unlock the door.' Apparently unaware of his response to her, she gave the order sharply, a note of panic in her voice. 'Unlock it now.'

'I take orders only from the Sultan himself.'

'Please…' Her face had lost most of its colour, and he frowned.

'You have just faced my blade without showing the slightest consideration for your personal safety,' he drawled softly. 'And yet you expect me to believe that you're afraid of a locked door?'

'Just open it,' she said in a hoarse voice. 'Please open it.'

Perplexed and exasperated in equal measure, Karim turned the key, watching as she relaxed. The rebel princess was afraid of a locked door? It was so incredibly unlikely that he almost laughed. If she was that easy to frighten then it should take very little to persuade her that life in the harsh climate of Zangrar, in the company of a ruthless Sultan, was definitely *not* for her.

'I don't fight women, Your Highness.'

She stilled and then gave a tiny shrug, some of her defiance returning. 'You do now.' With a single, graceful movement of her shoulders, she removed her jacket. 'And, anyway, you won. Your ego is still intact.'

'My ego requires no protection.' He dragged his eyes away from her hair with difficulty, his brain and body fighting a vicious battle for supremacy. Intellect warred with basic masculine instinct, and the sudden tightening of his body reminded him that the power of basic masculine instinct was never to be underestimated. 'I could have hurt you.'

Only now, when she stood without the thick, protective padding of the fencing jacket, could he see how fine-boned and delicately built she was. Her exquisitely perfect face revealed centuries of breeding, and Karim studied her closely, trying to reconcile the innocence of that face with her debauched reputation. And she studied him back, her gaze fearless and unfaltering.

Then she turned and hung her jacket in the cupboard. 'You're good. But you've had a wasted journey. I don't want a bodyguard.'

'Your wishes in the matter are irrelevant, Your Highness.' Whether she wanted him or not, she was getting him. His mission was to persuade her to change her mind about marrying the Sultan, and he needed to be with her on the journey if he was to achieve that goal.

Her glance was curious. 'Do you guard the Sultan himself?'

It wasn't a question he'd anticipated, and it took him a moment to formulate an acceptable answer. 'I have ultimate responsibility for the Sultan's safety, yes.'

'In that case, I'm sure he's missing you. Go home.' With a swift movement of her fingers, she removed the plastron, the half-jacket that protected her fencing arm. 'Use your talents elsewhere. I don't need them.'

'You are no longer planning to marry the Sultan?'

'Of course I'm marrying the Sultan. But I don't need anyone with me on the journey. I prefer to arrange my own protection.'

'And who have you selected to provide this service?'

'Me.' Her tone suggested that she considered the answer obvious. 'If there's one thing I've learned over the years, it's that, when it comes to safety issues, the only person you can really depend on is yourself.'

'You plan to travel through the desert alone and unaccompanied?'

'Absolutely. And I hope no one threatens me, because I'm lethal when I'm threatened.' As if determined to convince him of that fact, she fixed him with her cool, blue stare, and Karim lifted an eyebrow.

'Clearly you are unaware of the fact that many men find a woman's vulnerability to be one of her greatest charms.'

'Those same men undoubtedly have miniscule egos and need to slay dragons in order to demonstrate their masculinity.' She stooped to put her mask and glove in the cupboard. 'I refuse to put my safety at risk in order to pander to a man's need to flex his muscles in public. I slay my own dragons.'

For the first time in his adult life, Karim found himself speechless. He'd never met a woman like her before. 'You cannot seriously be intending to make the journey to Zangrar alone? You have no knowledge of the route.'

'I can read a map, use satellite navigation and I can talk on the phone. Princesses have a multitude of skills these days. We're a very versatile breed. Haven't you heard?'

What he'd heard was that the Princess Alexandra was a real rebel, and he could see that the rumours had foundation. There was a fire in her eyes and defiance in her stance, and even after five minutes in her company he could see that she was no man's idea of a gentle, compliant wife.

She was a handful.

Even while contemplating the disaster that would ensue if this woman ever arrived in Zangrar, Karim was reflecting on the fact that this next battle between them might be every bit as stimulating as the fencing. Removing his own jacket, he stretched out a hand and dropped it onto the nearest chair. 'Clearly you've never aspired to be like the princesses in the fairy stories.'

'Passive victims, you mean?' A thoughtful frown touched her forehead and then she gave a careless shrug. 'I wouldn't be stupid enough to take a poisoned apple from a stepmother who hates me, and I've always hated sewing, so there's no way I'd prick my finger on a spinning wheel.'

'But you *are* planning to marry a sultan,' Karim pointed out silkily, and she smiled, showing no signs of trepidation at the prospect.

'That's right. I am.'

'And the Sultan insists that you are escorted on the journey, Your Highness.'

The princess turned to face him, and their eyes locked in a battle of wills.

Supremely confident that there was only one possible outcome, Karim crossed his arms and waited.

And waited.

'Fine.' Her gaze slid from his, and she toed off her fencing shoes with a graceful movement. 'If you want to come along then I suppose I can't stop you. I just hope you don't regret it. Who is guarding the Sultan while you are watching over me?'

Surprised by the speed with which success had been achieved, Karim felt a flash of suspicion. *What was she up to?* 'His Excellency is presently on an important and most secret mission that relates to the future stability of Zangrar. His security is being handled—elsewhere.'

She put her shoes in the cupboard. 'You haven't told me your name.'

Distracted by the thrust of her breasts under the simple white tee-shirt, it took him a moment to answer. 'You may call me Karim, Your Highness.'

'And you may call me Alexa. I'm not big on protocol.'

Remembering everything he'd read about her lifestyle, Karim had little trouble believing that statement. 'It would not be appropriate for me to call you by your first name.'

'You weren't worrying about what was appropriate when you dragged me into this room.' Her gaze was speculative.

'Clearly you're a man accustomed to acting on your own initiative.'

'You want a bodyguard who waits for permission before saving you?'

'I don't want a bodyguard at all.' Tucking the last of her clothes into the cupboard, she slammed the door shut. 'If there's any saving to be done, then I prefer to do it myself. Let's get that straight before we leave this room.'

Karim clenched his jaw in order to refrain from pointing out that the only thing she needed saving from was *herself*. Only the month before she'd been removed unconscious from a nightclub, and he knew that she'd had at least two car crashes and a boating accident in the past year, and from all of them she'd narrowly escaped with her life. The Princess Alexandra was clearly as reckless as she was bold.

'The desert is full of dangers, many of which are concealed from all but those who were born and bred there.'

'I have lived with danger all my life. I have a question for you, Karim.' Without glancing in his direction, she slipped on a slim-fitting jumper in a deep shade of green. She still wore her fencing breeches, and he saw that her legs were long and slim.

'Ask your question.'

'How do you feel about the Sultan? Would you die for him?'

Karim reflected on the irony of that question. 'Without a doubt.'

Scooping up her hair, she pinned it haphazardly on top of her head, disregarding the fact that several strands immediately escaped and tumbled down around her face. 'And just how much do you know about *my* country, Karim?'

With perfect recall, Karim summarized the briefing he'd received. 'Rovina is a small principality ruled by your uncle, the Regent, who has been in power since your parents were killed in an accident. You were the only heir, and too young to ascend the throne.' He saw darkness flicker across her beautiful face, and wondered briefly whether that tragic event had been responsible for her wild behaviour. Without the guiding hand of a father, had she gone off the rails? 'Your late father and the Sultan's late father were friends, and made the agreement for you and the present sultan to wed when you reached the age of twenty-four. Your birthday is in four days.' Was it his imagination or was her breathing suddenly more rapid?

'You've done your homework.'

'One year after that, on the day of your twenty-fifth birthday, you will be crowned Queen of Rovina. Knowing that, I am intrigued as to why you would wish to move to a different continent and marry a man you've never even met, and whose culture and beliefs are so different from your own.' If he talked her out of the marriage now, he could save himself an arduous journey with a woman who was undoubtedly going to whine and moan her way across the baking desert, a climate not known for nurturing patience in those who experienced it.

'You don't think I should marry the Sultan?'

'On the contrary.' Karim issued the denial smoothly. 'I'm sure a marriage between you would be a great success. Your Highness is clearly both brave and bold, and you will need both qualities in abundance if you are to tame our sultan.'

'Tame?'

'I once heard a woman remark that the Sultan of Zangrar resembles a tiger who has been taken from the wild and forced to live in captivity.' Satisfied that he had her attention, Karim delivered what he hoped passed for a sympathetic smile. 'The woman who eventually shares his cage would have to be *particularly* courageous.'

Alexa laughed. 'If you're trying to frighten me, Karim, then you've picked the wrong woman.'

'I'm not trying to frighten you,' he lied, concealing his surprise at her laughter. 'On the contrary, the more I see of you, the greater my conviction that you are a match for the Sultan even in one of his most dangerous moods. I just wanted to be sure that you know your own mind. If you wish to back out of the agreement, then you may do so.'

'I *don't* wish that.'

As he stared into her wide, blue eyes he felt another powerful tug of chemistry followed by a vicious tightening in his groin as white-hot lust shot through him. He wondered whether it was too soon to inform her that there was only one way the Sultan would ever want her—and that was flat on her back, naked and *without* the wedding ring. 'Clearly, there is no place for love or romance in your life.'

Her beautiful blue eyes shone with genuine amusement. 'Are you telling me that you believe in love, Karim? Are you a romantic man?'

'This conversation is not about me.'

'Judging from your tone, I've touched on a sensitive subject.' She studied him in silence for a moment and then paced over to the window, her eyes flickering to the palace grounds. 'I'm not pretending this marriage has anything to do with love, because we both know that it doesn't…' Her words tailed off and she frowned, as if surprised at herself. 'Why am I telling you this? My reasons for wishing to marry the Sultan are not your concern. Your brief is simply to escort me safely to Zangrar.'

Karim wondered what she would say if she knew that his brief was a great deal more complex than that. The Princess Alexandra was the only one who could break this ridiculous agreement, and it was his personal responsibility to ensure that she did exactly that.

She was *not* a suitable wife for a sultan.

Her motive for the wedding was clearly greed, and the fact that greed alone was sufficient to compel her to marry a man of whom she knew nothing, sickened him. A woman like her would do untold damage to Zangrar, and threaten the enormous progress they had already made.

Clearly unaware that Karim's own objective was in direct conflict with hers, Alexa paced back and forth across the room, her eyes on the door as if she expected to be disturbed at any moment. 'So, if you insist on traveling with me, then you'd better tell me your plans for the journey.'

'We leave at dawn. The Sultan's private jet is waiting at the airport.'

Had he not been watching closely, he might have missed the way that her slender fingers suddenly locked and unlocked in a manifestly agitated gesture. *The princess was nervous about something.* The question was, *what?*

'My uncle is aware of those plans?'

As she turned to face him, he could almost feel her anxiety sharpening the atmosphere of the tiny room.

'He requested a full itinerary.'

'And you gave it to him. Excellent.' She was silent for a moment, apparently thinking. 'Then we leave at dawn. My uncle wishes you to join us for dinner. As the Sultan's envoy, you are the guest of honour. But I have one more question before we leave this room.'

'Ask it.'

'Are you truly good at your job, Karim? Are you really the best?'

'Your wellbeing is my highest priority, Your Highness. You have no reason to worry about your safety.'

Her laugh was hollow. 'You think not?'

Was she afraid of some sort of physical threat? Resolving to question the palace security-team in greater depth, Karim frowned. 'No one would dare lay a finger on the Sultan's future bride.'

The princess watched him for a long moment, her wide blue eyes fixed on his face with disturbing intensity. 'Except, perhaps, those who don't want me to be the Sultan's bride.'

CHAPTER TWO

ALEXA sat at the long table in the banqueting hall, her hands shaking so badly she could barely hold a knife and fork. She was so on edge that it was almost impossible to sit still. If it wasn't for the fact that her uncle would have become suspicious, she would have excused herself from dinner. As it was, she didn't dare. Too much was at stake.

Although she was staring at her plate, she nevertheless saw Karim's hand reach for his wine, and her attention was momentarily drawn to the strength of his long, bronzed fingers. Then his arm brushed against hers and that simple, innocent contact was enough to send heat rushing to her pelvis.

Instantly she shifted away from him, bewildered and alarmed by her inexplicable reaction to him. What was the matter with her? Why was her body selecting this particular moment to notice the finer points of the male physique? Had her mind elevated him to hero status simply because he'd insisted on remaining by her side for the journey? Surely not, when she knew perfectly well that having him there was going to threaten everything that she'd been working towards.

She needed to be the one in charge, and she definitely couldn't risk having some autocratic, commanding bodyguard thinking that he knew what was best for her. And she *certainly* wasn't going to do anything as foolish as trusting anyone with her future.

'You're unusually quiet, Alexa.' Her uncle William's cultured tones cut through the murmur of conversation around the table, and he raised his glass to Karim. 'I hope you have decent shops in Zangrar. Alexa isn't going to be happy somewhere that doesn't have shops. All that glitters has to be gold, that's her motto—isn't that right, my sweet?'

Knowing from experience that her uncle was always at his most deadly when he used his caring voice, Alexa felt a flutter of panic and focused on the subtle flex of muscle in Karim's forearm as he returned his glass to the table.

She hoped he was as tough as he looked. He'd unwittingly landed himself right in the middle of palace crossfire with no flak jacket to protect him, and she knew that if he happened to be standing between her and her uncle when the final moment came then he'd die alongside her.

Her conscience nagged her.

Why hadn't he just gone home as she'd ordered?

She hadn't wanted to drag anyone else into this.

Aware that her uncle was watching her, Alexa faked a yawn and tried to look like a girl incapable of planning anything other than her next shopping trip. 'I've heard that some of the souks sell amazing silks. I'm looking forward to designing myself a whole new wardrobe.'

'I admit that I've probably overindulged her a little since her parents were killed.' William addressed his remark to Karim. 'I just hope that the Sultan will be as generous as he is wealthy.'

'The Sultan's generosity is not in question, but it is hard to spend money in the desert, and that is where much of his time is currently spent.' Karim spoke in a matter-of-fact voice and Alexa turned her head and looked at him, unable to hide her surprise.

'He lives in the desert?'

'Since the death of his father, the Sultan has spent much of his time in the desert with his people. His wife will be expected to support him in that role. If you wish to augment your wardrobe, you might be wise to include robes and sturdy desert-boots.' He reached for his glass. 'The sort that repel the bite of a snake.'

Reflecting on the fact that dealing with snakes would be a piece of cake after living with her uncle for sixteen years, Alexa gave a shrug. 'I'm sure I can live in the desert if I have to. I mean, when all is said and done, it's just a giant beach, really. Sand, sand and more sand.' She kept her tone as light as the subject matter. 'I'm sure the Sultan isn't going to want his wife dressed in rags. With all that money at his disposal, he's hardly going to begrudge me a few pairs of shoes.'

William's eyes narrowed. 'He might, when he finds out how much they cost! Karim, I've been telling my niece that this marriage is ridiculous. Her father arranged it when she was a child, before he had any idea what sort of a woman she would become. And the truth is that she is *not* a woman who is going to be happy incarcerated in a dusty old fortress in the middle of a baking-hot desert.' He softened his words with a smile and reached for his wine. 'No offence.'

Alexa felt Karim's sudden stillness, and wondered whether it was possible to die of embarrassment.

Reminding herself that Karim's thoughts and feelings had to be secondary to William's, she forced the expected response from her mouth. 'I'm sure the Sultan entertains occasionally. As long as there's a party going on, and everyone is having a good time, it doesn't really matter where it is.' Out of the corner of her eyes, she saw Karim's long, strong fingers tighten on the stem of his glass.

'Parties are not high on the Sultan's agenda. When he entertains, the guest list includes foreign dignitaries and other heads of state. The purpose of the gathering is all about diplomacy and international relations.'

He obviously thought she was shallow-minded and frivolous, which didn't surprise her. What did surprise her was the fact that she minded what he thought. Why would she care about the opinions of a bodyguard? His views were irrelevant. They *had* to be. Tonight of all nights it was essential that she maintained her image of a woman who thought about nothing deeper than what to wear at her next social engagement. If William knew what was truly on her mind, he would be turning all of the keys in all of the doors.

'Foreign dignitaries sound pretty dull.' She suppressed a yawn. 'I'm sure I'll be able to help the Sultan liven things up a bit.'

William's gaze flickered from her to Karim. 'Her head is full of romance. She's expecting Arab stallions, a desert and a glamorous Sultan who is going to sweep her off her expensively clad feet.'

Aware that the expression on Karim's face had gone from mild impatience to thunderous disapproval, Alexa wondered if he was about to lose his temper.

Her heart thumping against her chest, she braced herself for a terrifying display of masculine aggression—but when he finally spoke Karim's tone seemed almost bored.

'There is nothing romantic about the desert. It is a harsh, unforgiving landscape that contains any number of threats. A sandstorm is one of the most deadly natural phenomena known to man, and the desert in Zangrar is inhabited by scorpions and snakes so dangerous that one bite produces sufficient venom to kill ten grown men.'

'Scorpions and snakes. You see, Alexa?' William leaned back, and someone hastily stepped forward to remove his plate. 'It is a long way from Rovina.'

'Indeed, it is,' Alexa said quietly. *She was banking on it.* 'Nevertheless, my father arranged this marriage, and I shall do as he wished. I owe it to his memory.'

And she owed it to the people of Rovina. The only way she

was ever going to reach her twenty-fifth birthday was if she married the Sultan.

Karim's dark gaze fixed on her with brooding intensity. 'You are very young, Your Highness. Your uncle is obviously worrying about how you will fare in a country like Zangrar. You would do well to listen to his advice.'

'I'm not afraid of anything I'll find in Zangrar.'

'Then perhaps you are not sufficiently enlightened as to exactly what awaits you.' He spoke softly, his words only audible to her, and she lifted her gaze to his, wondering what he was alluding to.

Their eyes met and held, and Alexa felt a shiver of awareness and a flash of the same sexual chemistry that had singed her earlier in the day. 'You're doing it again—trying to frighten me.'

He lifted a dark eyebrow in sardonic appraisal. '*Are* you frightened, Your Highness?'

'No.' *But that was only because she knew what true fear was.*

Alexa glanced across the table at William and saw him smiling at her. Her pulse-rate doubled. If the Sultan's bodyguard really wanted to know what frightened her, then he need look no further than the man sitting across from them. Over the years she'd learned to read her uncle's moods, and if there was one thing that scared her more than his temper it was his smile.

His smile widened as he looked at her. 'I hear she fenced you earlier, Karim. Hardly a ladylike sport, I'm sure you'll agree. I think you're going to find that the Princess Alexandra is unusual in many ways. Most of the time you wouldn't even know she was a princess, from the way she behaves.'

Alexa noticed the sudden tightening of Karim's mouth, and knew that William's repeated attempts to undermine her were succeeding. Not for the first time in her life, she was seriously tempted to pick up her knife and silence her uncle in the most permanent way possible.

'I have many qualities which the Sultan will appreciate,' she said lightly, and then saw the glimmer of disdain in the bodyguard's eyes and realized that she'd actually made the situation worse, not better.

Not those qualities! she wanted to shout. Why were men so basic? Why did they only *ever* think about one thing—sex? Well, actually, it was two things. Sex and power. Forget everything else—they seemed to be the only two things that motivated the male species.

And normally she didn't even *think* about sex. So why was it that, since the Sultan's bodyguard had removed his fencing mask and revealed his impossibly handsome face, she'd thought about little else?

Or perhaps it was just that this whole situation was turning her slowly loopy. There was so much at stake. *And so many things that could still go wrong.*

She was a nervous wreck.

Marrying the Sultan was the only way that Rovina would have a future, and if anything happened to prevent that...

Reminding herself that this was *not* the time to lose her cool, she allowed herself a small sip of wine.

William gave her a sympathetic smile. 'Talking of qualities, most of yours are displayed over the front page of today's newspapers. I think the headline read something like, "rebel princess hot for the harem?" I mean, really—' he gave a weary shake of his head '—newspapers have no sense of moral restraint. Always digging up the past when it should be forgotten. We just have to hope for your sake that the Sultan isn't expecting a virgin bride. Perhaps his reputation is way off the mark and he's one of those rare men who values experience over innocence. I'm *so* sorry, Alexa.'

So was she.

Under no illusions as to why the papers had chosen to reprint those pictures, anger suddenly burst through her usual cautious restraint. 'When the time comes, I intend to tell the Sultan the truth about my life. *The whole truth,* Uncle William. And he *will* believe me.' She caught Karim's astonished glance and saw the deadly gleam light her uncle's eyes.

The emotion drained out of her, and she started to shake.

Why had she said that?

She'd gained *nothing* by that remark. Nothing at all. And she could have lost everything.

This was *not* the time to antagonize a man as dangerous as her uncle, and she knew that. Since when had she allowed anger to incinerate common sense?

'You're my niece,' William said smoothly. 'I only want what is best for you, and Zangrar is such a terribly long way away. I'm so afraid that something dreadful might happen to you on your journey. You know how accident prone you are.'

Alexa felt her heart stumble and her palms grow damp. *He was threatening her.*

'Karim will ensure my safety,' she said in a clear voice, hoping desperately that Karim wouldn't choose this moment to mention the fact that she'd tried to dispense with his services.

William gently dabbed his mouth with his napkin. 'If anything were to happen to you, I don't know what I'd do.'

He would have achieved his lifelong ambition.

He would finally have destroyed her family.

Suddenly Alexa felt bitterly cold. 'Your care and concern is always touching, Uncle William. My father would have become quite emotional, had he been able to see everything you've done for me since his death.' Unable to share his table a moment longer, she rose to her feet. 'We leave in the morning. I need my passport.' And this was the moment she'd been dreading.

For sixteen years he'd held her passport.

Would he finally return it to her?

William was silent for a long moment, and then he gave a gentle smile. 'You are such a featherbrain. I will give it to Karim for safekeeping.'

No, no, *no!*

Her stomach turned over. She *had* to have her passport. And the fact that William was prepared to give it to Karim was of no use to her at all, because she knew that he had no intention of allowing her to leave in the morning.

Which was why she had no intention of waiting until morning.

Alexa felt a great weight in her chest. So much depended on the next few hours. If she couldn't gain possession of her passport, then she couldn't take the next step and everything would have been for nothing.

Trying to think her way through the dark mists of panic, she tried to look relaxed. 'That's fine. Give my passport to Karim.'

One way or another she would just have to find a way of retrieving it.

She just hoped the bodyguard was a heavy sleeper.

The room was dark but she could see the faint outline of his body lying under the covers. He was asleep, thank goodness. She'd been relying on that fact.

Where was he likely to have put her passport?

Seeing his jacket on the back of a chair, she moved towards it with the stealth of a burglar, her bare feet making no sound on the carpet. She reached out a hand, and then gasped with shock as someone caught her from behind, unbalanced her and pushed her down hard onto the bed. Flattened against the mattress and panicking, Alexa fought like an animal in a trap, using all the skills she'd learned to defend herself. She twisted, bit and punched, but as her fist connected with solid muscle she realized desperately that this was a hopelessly uneven contest, and she was going to lose.

No! This wasn't going to happen to her. Not when she was so

close to her final goal. Driven by desperation, she managed to free one leg and kicked hard.

With a grunt of pain, her assailant shifted his body over hers, caught her wrists in a vice-like grip and muttered something in a foreign language.

She recognized the voice. 'Karim?'

She felt him still, and then he pinned her to the bed with his powerful body and reached out a hand to flick on the light.

Alexa found herself staring into dark pools of anger and went limp with relief. 'I thought—'

'You thought what? You were expecting someone else?' He stared down at her with incredulous disbelief. 'This is *my* bedroom.'

'Yes, I know that.' The weight of his body made it hard for her to breathe. 'But I saw the lump in the bed and assumed you were asleep. Then someone grabbed me from behind so I thought it was—' She broke off, unwilling to betray more than she had to.

'The lump in the bed was the pillow. I heard you outside the door. I wanted to see who was so keen to enter my bedroom un-announced. What is this, Your Highness—you are now testing me in unarmed combat, or did you have an entirely different reason for visiting me in my bedroom in the middle of the night?' His meaning was clear enough, and suddenly she was breathlessly aware of the strength in his bare shoulders, of the intimate pressure of his body against hers.

'I need my passport. *That* is why I was in your bedroom.'

'Why would you need your passport at three in the morning? Are you planning a trip?'

She tried to wriggle free, but his weight held her pinned to the mattress. 'It's none of your business.'

'If it involves your passport, then it's my business.'

Alexa tried a different tack. 'The Sultan would *not* want you lying on top of his bride!'

'Given that I'm apparently just one in a long line of men who have adopted this exact position, I think it's a little late for that argument to be useful.' His soft tone was faintly mocking. 'My job is to escort you safely to him. If you're intending to vanish in the middle of the night, then your travel plans are of considerable interest to me. Start talking, Your Highness.'

The weight of his body was impossibly distracting, and Alexa suddenly found that she couldn't say a word. Trapped by his virile strength and the fire in his eyes, she just gazed at him, her body paralyzed by a shockingly powerful explosion of sexual excitement.

And perhaps he detected her feelings, because he shifted slightly above her, his attitude softening from aggressor to seducer.

Alexa pressed her hand to his chest intending to push him away, but her fingertips registered warm, naked flesh. Male body-hair and hard muscle singed her nerve endings, but instead of pushing or even drawing her hand away, her fingers made their own decision and slid upwards, exploring the latent power of his physique with unconscious feminine fascination.

Karim inhaled sharply and growled something that she didn't understand.

And then they were kissing.

His mouth was demanding and fiercely possessive, and her body ignited like a dry forest in the heat of summer as every single part of her was sucked in by the ferocious heat generated by that kiss.

She felt the hot slide of his tongue against hers, and the erotic intimacy of that connection drained her body of strength and purpose. She forgot what she was doing in his room. She forgot *everything* as her body was filled with a languorous, dangerous warmth, and his kiss transformed her from a thinking woman to someone only capable of feeling.

Dimly, she registered the hardness of his body against hers and the steady thud of his heartbeat under her clinging fingers.

And then suddenly he dragged his mouth from hers and lifted

his head, his breathing uneven and his eyes angry. '*What* do you think you are doing?'

Dizzy and drugged, it took a moment to focus. '*You* kissed *me*.'

'*Your* hands were on *my* body.'

Unable to defend herself from the accusation, Alexa lay there in shock, trying to work out what had happened. Kissing Karim had been like stepping into sexual quicksand—one move in the wrong place and she hadn't been able to free herself. Every subtle movement of his mouth had just drawn her down deeper until she'd drowned, swallowed up by pleasure and sensation.

Why was that?

Had the agonizing loneliness of her situation finally affected her mind? Was she so desperate for human comfort that she was ready to cling to any man who touched her?

'Please, let me go. I just want my passport.' Her voice was shaking. How had she allowed herself to become so distracted from her task? The clock was ticking. Every moment that passed made her task more dangerous. 'Let me leave tonight without you. You will not be blamed.'

Karim studied her face for a moment and then sprang to his feet in a lithe, athletic movement, relieving her of his weight so suddenly that she felt unaccountably bereft.

Ignoring the confusion in her brain and body, Alexa sat up and than gave a gulp of shock she realized that he was completely naked—*gloriously, proudly naked, and unashamedly aroused.*

She knew she should look away but she couldn't move. Confronted by her first ever vision of a naked man, her eyes remained fixed on this impromptu display of rampant masculinity, and only when she heard his sharply indrawn breath did she finally manage to drag her eyes upwards. But, instead of respite, she was offered just another angle on impressive manhood—wide, powerful shoulders, curving muscles honed by hard physical exercise and a broad, strong chest hazed by curling dark hairs. He was aggressively, imposingly masculine, and it took all her willpower to look away from such physical perfection. Her cheeks were burning, and she honestly didn't know what to say or do to move on from here. Her head had emptied itself of all thoughts that weren't related to sex with this man.

No wonder she hadn't been able to resist his kiss.

'The blushing is sweet, but a little over the top given the kiss we just shared.' Karim's tone was icy cold as he reached for the robe that was flung carelessly over the chair. Without any obvious sign of haste, he slid his arms into the sleeves and belted it loosely, as relaxed and cool as she was embarrassed. 'And your display of shyness is a little out of place in a woman who began exploring her sexuality at such a young age—but if you want to play that game then I'm happy to oblige. It's safe to look, Your Highness.'

Safe?

Part of her knew that this man was anything *but* safe, and the knowledge unsettled her more than she cared to admit. She'd lived with the threat of danger all her life, but this was *entirely* different. Normally she was completely in control of her reactions, but with Karim she wasn't in control at all and the thought terrified her. She couldn't afford to be distracted. She didn't *need* this confusion. Her mind needed to be sharp and focused.

Her future depended on it.

The future of Rovina depended on it.

Her cheeks still flaming with embarrassment, Alexa struggled to find some of her old, rational self. Part of her wanted to melt from the room and never see him again, but another part wanted to…

'None of that is important,' she said hoarsely, saying it for her own benefit as much as his. 'I—'

'You what?' He folded his arms and fixed her with his hard, unsympathetic gaze. 'The Sultan would not approve of the conduct of his prospective bride. He's an *extremely* possessive man.'

'We both know that the Sultan is unlikely to care what happens to me.'

Since when had *anyone* cared what happened to her? She'd been surviving on her own for so long that it was impossible to imagine a scenario where she mattered to someone.

'You're wrong.' Karim studied her with grim contemplation. 'If you marry him then you become his possession, and he's ruthlessly protective of anything and *everything* that is his. The ability to share nicely is not a virtue to which he aspires.'

She stood up, because sitting down made him all the more intimidating and she couldn't think straight when she was facing him. 'You've stumbled into a situation that you know nothing about. Believe me, if you'd known the facts, there is no *way* you would have signed up for this job. Just let me go and perhaps we'll meet up in Zangrar one day.' *If she survived the journey.* She turned and caught the narrowing of his eyes.

'So, your uncle kept your passport from you. Presumably for your own good. You're clearly something of a handful to manage, Your Highness. I don't envy him.'

Alexa straightened her shoulders. 'Your role is not to pass judgement on a situation of which you know nothing. It's not your business.'

'If you're planning to sneak away then it becomes my business. If I wake up tomorrow and you have gone then I will have to answer to the Sultan. His Excellency isn't exactly renowned for tolerating the mistakes of others.'

'Coming with me would be a bigger mistake than you can possibly imagine.'

'If you believe that then you clearly know nothing about the Sultan.' He walked towards her, his expression unreadable. 'If you disappear while under my protection then it is entirely my responsibility.'

'The Sultan wouldn't care. He doesn't want this marriage.'

'Nor does he want an international incident,' Karim said dryly. 'Make no mistake, the Sultan is going ahead with this marriage. The plans for the wedding are already underway. You marry him on the day of your twenty-fourth birthday.'

'Yes, but I intend to travel alone. If you refuse to let me go, then you *will* regret it.'

A muscle worked in his lean jaw, and his eyes were faintly amused as he surveyed her with disturbing thoroughness. 'Never before have I been threatened by a woman who barely reaches my shoulder.'

Alexa felt exhaustion wash over her. As if it wasn't enough to constantly be trying to outwit William, she now had another fight on her hands. Utterly defeated by the constant obstacles that faced her, she sank back onto the edge of the bed, and then noticed something glinting under the edge of the pillow.

Puzzled, she reached out a hand, lifted the pillow and gave a soft gasp. 'You sleep with a gun and a knife?'

'I'm a cautious man.' He walked over to the bed and gently prised her fingers from the pillow before dragging her back to her feet. 'And I want to know *why* you feel the need to leave the palace in the middle of the night.'

She tried to ignore the fact that his hand still held hers. 'Because it's imperative that I reach Zangrar safely.'

He watched her for a long moment. 'You're that desperate to marry the Sultan?'

'I prefer *determined* to *desperate*.' *Although desperate was probably much closer to the truth.*

'And you believe that your uncle is going to try and stop you?'

'If I wait until morning—yes.' Alexa hesitated but decided that she had no choice but to tell him at least part of the truth.

'William feels very strongly that this wedding shouldn't go ahead. Strongly enough to use physical means to prevent it.'

Karim was silent for a moment as he digested that piece of information. 'He must love you very much to have such strong concerns for your well-being. And yet you choose to ignore that love?'

Alexa stared at him for a moment and then gave a short laugh. 'He doesn't love me. He hates me. He has always hated me.'

'You're young. Sometimes, when someone else's wishes for you are in contrast to your own, it can be hard to hear what they are saying.'

'There's nothing wrong with my hearing. My uncle isn't interested in what's best for me.' She eyed the door, knowing that she was wasting precious minutes that she didn't have. 'I have to go.'

'If you leave, then I leave. Make no mistake about that. I'm your bodyguard.'

'Haven't you listened to a word I've said? I don't need you.'

'Why not, if you think you're at risk?'

'I don't trust you.'

Karim frowned. 'What possible reason could there be for you not to trust me?'

'I don't trust anyone. And if you insist on coming on this journey then I certainly can't guarantee your safety.'

One dark eyebrow lifted in mockery. 'I rather thought that *I* was supposed to guarantee *your* safety.'

She sighed and rubbed her aching head with the tips of her fingers. 'Karim, I'm *not* a good person to travel with. It is going to be dangerous.'

'Don't you think you're being a little melodramatic?'

He had no idea. Alexa let her hands drop to her sides and gave a resigned shrug. She'd already wasted too much time on this. She'd warned him. If he chose to ignore the warning, then that was up to him. 'I'm leaving now, whether you come or not is up to you,' she said wearily. 'But, if you wait until the morning, then I'll be gone, with or without the passport. And, if *I* wait until morning, I'll be dead. In case you haven't heard, I'm very accident-prone.'

She heard his sharp intake of breath as she walked across the room. At the door she paused and turned to look at him. 'If you're coming with me then bring the gun and the knife—and I just hope you're as good as you say you are, because you're about to need every survival skill you've ever learned.'

CHAPTER THREE

KARIM slid into the tiny car, wondering at precisely which point in the past twenty-four hours he'd relinquished grip on his judgement.

He brushed the tips of his fingers over his lower lip, trying to erase the delicious taste of her mouth and the memory of that searing kiss, but the gesture did nothing to alleviate the nagging ache of lust that now gripped his body.

Intensely irritated by his own response, he let his hand fall to his thigh.

She was the most hotly sexual woman he'd ever met, and her behaviour was every bit as shocking as he'd been led to believe.

The fact that she was prepared to kiss another man days before her wedding confirmed everything he already knew about her, and that kiss had obviously shorted his mental circuits because he was behaving in a way that was entirely uncharacteristic. Instead of being fully in control of the situation, he was now on his way to a mystery destination with a princess who gave new meaning to the term *drama queen*.

Dead. *Dead?*

What did she mean that if she waited until morning she'd be *dead*?

Clearly, she thought a little exaggeration on her part would help urge him into action, or perhaps she'd just been aiming for the sympathy vote. It was a pity for her that he had vast experience of a woman's ability to manipulate a tricky situation to her advantage, especially where money was involved. Obviously the Princess Alexandra was afraid that her uncle might step in and prevent the wedding. And it didn't need a genius to work out why she would go to any lengths to prevent that happening.

Money had an appalling effect on people. He'd seen it firsthand, and her determination to creep away from the palace in the middle of the night in order to protect her prize, had left him with no obvious alternative but to join her. Until she changed her mind about the marriage, his mission was not complete, and his mission stood no chance of being completed if she travelled to Zangrar alone and unaccompanied.

He needed time with her.

Wincing as his shoulders brushed the door and his head banged the roof, Karim tried to shift himself into a more comfortable position, but it proved impossible. 'I'm surprised you didn't opt for a more luxurious mode of transport,' he muttered, but she didn't even glance in his direction.

'I'm not interested in luxury. I'm interested in anonymity.'

Well aware that that both those statements were in direct contrast to everything he knew about the Princess Alexandra's public displays of extravagance, Karim wondered what she was trying to prove by making him journey in the smallest car available to mankind.

A road-sign flashed past and he frowned. 'You took the wrong road. The airport is the other way.'

She didn't respond. Instead her eyes were fixed on the road, and her hands gripped the wheel of the car so tightly that her knuckles whitened under the pressure. 'We're not using that airport.'

'The Sultan's private jet awaits you at Rovina Airport.'

'I know. Which makes it the first place they'll look when they realize that we've gone.' She glanced in her rear-view mirror and then turned left down a road without indicating. Tyres screeched in protest, and Karim's shoulder thudded hard against the window.

Watching his life flash before his eyes, he inhaled sharply. '*Stop* the car! I will drive.'

'No way. For a start, you don't know where we're going.'

'True. But, wherever it is, I would like to reach there alive.' He adjusted his balance as she took sharp right that virtually flung him on top of her.

'You chose to come, Karim.' She changed gears like a racing driver. 'Are you a nervous passenger?'

'That depends on the driver.'

'I'm an *excellent* driver.'

'And yet you have crawled from the wreckage of two car accidents in the past year.'

'Precisely. A less skilled driver than me would have been killed.'

'A more skilled driver than you wouldn't have crashed in the first place. Why do you keep looking in the mirror? It's pitch-dark out there. There is nothing to see.'

'So far. I need to make sure that no one is following us.'

'Who would be following us?' Karim felt a flicker of irritation. 'Some women are incredibly aroused by drama, I know, but you are taking it to new levels. Stop the car.'

'No. There's a chance that my uncle may have discovered that we've left. If I stop, then I risk losing the advantage we have.'

'Has it ever occurred to you that your uncle may have your best interests at heart?'

'Has it ever occurred to you that he hasn't? Don't lecture me, Karim. You're the one who insisted that I needed a bodyguard. I wanted to leave you behind.' She changed gears smoothly and accelerated fast up a dark road. There were no lights at all, but she seemed to know every bend and curve. 'You chose to come with me. That means that you go where I go.'

'And where is that, precisely?'

'I'm going to the Sultan. By my own route.'

'I hope that you will not have cause to regret that decision.' Her determination exasperated him. Why was it that women became so focused when faced with an increase in their fortunes?

'My father wanted me to marry the Sultan.'

'Your father had never met the present Sultan.'

'True. But he knew his father.'

Karim felt something dark and dangerous curl inside him. 'Perhaps I should inform you that you might find that the present Sultan is not such a soft touch when it comes to a pretty face.'

'It doesn't matter. We both know that the Sultan cannot break the contract that exists between us.'

'I'm sure the Sultan will find your eagerness to wed him most flattering.'

'There's no need for sarcasm. We've already established that I'm not pretending to be in love with him, and from what I've read that should be a pleasant change for the man,' she muttered, crunching the gears as she slowed fractionally to take a corner. 'He seems to spend his life fending off over-eager women. It must be very frustrating for him.'

'You needn't waste sympathy on the Sultan,' Karim drawled. 'He has vast experience with women, and is well able to protect himself.'

'Well, he won't need to protect himself from me. I'm honest.' She trod hard on the accelerator. 'And I certainly won't be pretending to be in love with him. We're going to get along just fine.'

'I'm sure the Sultan will be overwhelmed by your romantic nature,' Karim said dryly, wondering whether greed was any less distasteful when it was practised openly.

'From what I've heard, the Sultan doesn't have a romantic bone in his body.'

'You're very sure about that. What if marriage to you is preventing him from marrying someone else?'

'Oh, come on, Karim! You yourself said that the Sultan has avoided marriage all his life. He's thirty-four years old, and he's dated every beautiful woman in the western hemisphere.' She changed gears viciously. 'If there was someone he wanted to marry, he would have done it by now.'

'And you have reached this conclusion on what basis?'

'He's the Sultan. The absolute ruler. He can marry anyone he pleases.'

'Evidently not, since it seems that he will be marrying you. I'm afraid life is nowhere near as simple as you describe, even for the Sultan.'

'We're here.' Ignoring his last remark, she turned the wheel sharply and drove the car through a gap in a fence and into an open field. Then she flashed the headlights three times. From across the field came an answering flash, and she nodded and switched off the engine. 'We need to be quick.'

She was already out of the vehicle, the collar of her black jacket pulled up and a hat pulled low over her eyes. 'Hurry. I don't know how much time we have.'

Seriously questioning his decision to go along with her, Karim followed her, and then reached out a hand and hauled her against him. 'Enough,' he growled. '*Enough,* Your Highness. *No one is following us.*'

'Maybe not yet, but they will be. We need to get on that plane. Now.' Her voice was urgent. 'They're coming, Karim. They're already on their way. I can feel it.'

Karim felt her shiver in his arms, and his own body stirred in response as he stared down into her beautiful face. *Why was she so desperate to go through with this marriage? Was this really all about money?*

And what had happened to his judgement? Was he seriously going to board a strange aircraft with a woman who he didn't trust, like or even admire?

'You're making no sense. Give me one good reason why I should do as you say.'

Her breath was coming in rapid pants, and then she jerked away from him and pointed a gun—*his* gun—straight at his chest. 'Because if you don't then I'm just going to have to shoot you. I will not allow *anyone* to stop this marriage, and that includes you. We've already wasted far too much time. Make your choice, Karim, but make it fast.'

Her hands shaking, Alexa held the gun as she'd seen it held in the movies, hoping that she looked suitably threatening. 'Well?'

Karim stood still, remarkably calm, given that he was staring down the barrel of his own gun. And then he reached out and gently prised the gun from her shaking fingers with a hand that was entirely steady.

'It's dangerous to play with weapons that you know nothing about,' he said softly, and she made a desperate grab for the gun but he slid it back into the holster under his jacket. 'Next time you want to threaten someone, choose a weapon you're familiar with.' He watched her for a moment, his eyes searching. 'Given that our prompt departure is obviously a matter of great importance to you, we'd better leave.'

'Thank you.' She should have felt relief, but instead she found herself wishing that he'd opted to stay behind. He was the most disturbing man she'd ever met, and she didn't want him in her life. Especially not at this particular moment when concentration was crucial to her very survival. Alexa took a phone out of her pocket and made a quick call. Immediately a set of landing lights illuminated a runway, and she saw the small plane waiting. 'They're ready. Quickly.'

Checking over her shoulder for any glimmer of approaching headlights, Alexa pulled away from him and sprinted towards the plane, not really caring whether Karim followed or not.

She didn't understand why he was asking so many questions.

He was a bodyguard. His brief should have been to follow orders, not to give them.

Arriving at the plane, she climbed the few steps and then sank down on the nearest seat, her insides churning so badly that she could barely breath. Karim sat down next to her and she felt the brush of his arm against hers.

Even without turning her head she knew he was watching her. She could *feel* him watching her.

And then he gave an impatient sigh, leaned across and fastened her seat belt in a decisive movement. Wishing he'd selected a seat across the aisle, Alexa's mouth dried.

'Thank you.'

She didn't look at him. She didn't dare.

She had to stay focused, and looking at Karim just blurred her mind.

A man walked out of the cockpit and nodded to her. 'You are ready, Your Highness?'

'Yes. Just go, David. Quickly.' Knowing the risk he was taking, she looked at him doubtfully. 'You're sure you want to do this?'

'How can you doubt it?' The man's expression was fierce. 'We owe it to your father's memory. We owe it to Rovina.'

Karim lounged in the leather seat, studying the woman next to him through half-shuttered eyes.

The moment the plane had taken off, she'd fallen deeply asleep, and now she lay without moving, her thick, dark lashes forming a crescent against her ashen cheeks.

He still hadn't quite recovered from the shock of seeing her standing there, pointing his gun at him. But the incident had taught him two important things.

Firstly, that the Princess Alexandra was determined to marry the Sultan, and, secondly that she was not such a tough, independent soul as she would have liked him to believe. The slender hands holding his gun had been shaking so badly that, had she actually succeeded in firing the thing, the first shot would have hit his head and the second his toes. Clearly she didn't have a clue how to use a gun.

Still, he'd underestimated her, and he wouldn't be doing that again in a hurry.

Her extreme behaviour had surprised even him.

But it shouldn't have done, should it? He gave a cynical laugh. His wealth of experience with her sex had long since taught him that nothing focused a woman's mind more than a serious threat to her spending power, and the princess appeared to be facing that threat in the form of her uncle.

What would she say, he wondered, if she knew that he, too, was determined to prevent the wedding? The only difference between him and her uncle was that *he* intended to succeed.

Transferring his gaze to the front of the plane, he briefly wondered about the identity of the pilot. He'd been surprised by the loyalty and devotion displayed by the young man. Was he one of her many lovers?

Probably, if her reputation was to be believed.

Not that there had been any communication between them since that first brief greeting.

On the contrary, she'd been sleeping since the plane had taken off.

Deciding that it was time to take back control, Karim took advantage of her unconscious state to make some necessary calls. Blessing modern technology, he removed his hand-held computer from his pocket and sent two urgent e-mails that were both immediately answered. He was just pocketing the device when Alexa's head flopped sideways onto his shoulder.

Karim froze in shock as she snuggled into him. The top of her head brushed his neck as she automatically searched for the most comfortable position, and his senses were engulfed by the delicious scent of her amazing red-gold hair.

She smelt like an English garden in the middle of summer.

Seriously discomforted by the unexpected familiarity, he lifted a hand, intending to push her back into her own seat, but somehow his fingers became entwined in a lock of her hair. The curl looped itself around his fingers like a silken coil, and he studied the vibrancy of the colour with fascination.

Whatever else had been said about her, it was certainly true that the Princess Alexandra was astonishingly beautiful. She was a woman that any healthy, red-blooded man would find impossible to ignore. And as for how she tasted...

Irritated by the dangerous direction of his thoughts, Karim allowed her hair to slide through his fingers, reminding himself that this journey was all about helping her to review her decision to marry the Sultan. To stray from that path would complicate things in the extreme.

The weight and warmth of her body remained pressed against his shoulder, and, although sleeping snuggled against him was an intimacy he'd never before allowed a woman, Karim found himself strangely reluctant to wake her. He had no desire to travel with a tired, irritable woman, he reasoned, and anyway sleep not induced by the exhaustion of sex held no significance whatsoever.

He forced himself to relax in his seat, grimly determined to ignore the intrusive and disturbing reaction of his body. Occasionally he glanced at her, wondering when she was going to wake up.

She slept as though she was never going to regain consciousness, and at one point he found himself leaning closer, just to check that she was actually breathing.

It was only when the plane finally landed in Zangrar that she stirred, perhaps sensing the sudden stillness of the plane. Her head was still resting on his shoulder and her gaze met his, her face dangerously close.

Karim felt something stir inside him and curved his hand around her cheek, tempted to help himself to another taste of her luscious mouth before continuing with the job in hand. His body throbbed and ached with the memory of that kiss, and he realized with no small degree of irritation that he had been in an almost permanent state of arousal since he had met the princess only a day earlier. Only the most ruthless self-discipline prevented him from sacrificing his principles in favour of immediate sexual gratification. His hand dropped and he drew back, and she did the same, apparently dismayed to find herself so intimately entwined with him.

'I slept—I'm sorry.' She sounded astonished. 'What time is it?'

'We have just landed in Zangrar.'

'Landed?' Her expression confused, she looked out of the window. 'But that isn't possible.'

'*Why* isn't it possible?'

'Because Zangrar is a ten-hour flight.'

'And you have slept for ten hours.' *And for most of those ten hours she'd been wrapped around him.* Trying to calm the vicious throb in his body by moving his thoughts as far from seduction as possible, Karim flexed his shoulders. 'It was the middle of the night when we left. It is hardly surprising that you were tired.'

She looked shocked. 'I've slept for *ten hours?*'

'Without waking.'

'But I've never—' Without bothering to finish her sentence, she chewed her lip and glanced out of the window. 'So, if this is Zangrar, then how far is it to the Citadel?'

Karim gave a cynical smile. For single-minded focus, you couldn't fault her. She'd barely rubbed the sleep from her eyes, but already she could see the flash of gold across the desert. He only wished that half the people he worked with were even a fraction as driven. 'I'm sure the Sultan will be most flattered by your eagerness to begin married life.'

It was a moment before she replied, and he wondered whether she'd even heard his comment. Then she looked at him, her face blank of expression. 'I need somewhere to change. I can't wear this.'

'This' was the pair of dark trousers and black jumper that she'd worn to leave the palace, presumably chosen to disguise her identity. Clearly she wanted to change into something more glamorous before she met the Sultan.

'The Sultan is going to be far more interested in the person than the clothes. In Zangrar we have a tradition,' he said softly. 'When a woman marries, she dresses in a very simple gown, and that simplicity is of great significance. It means that she is offering herself to her man, all that she is, unadorned and exposed. It is symbolic of the fact that truth can be concealed, and that the marriage of a man and a woman should be about openness and truth.'

'Truth?' Her eyes fixed on his face. 'You're suggesting that I'm not being honest?'

'I'm saying that when a woman gives herself to a man there should be nothing concealed.'

'And what about when a man gives himself to a woman? How much concealing is allowed then? Or is this honesty one-sided?' Disillusionment rang in her voice, and the expression in her eyes was bleak. 'You still haven't answered my question. How far is the Citadel from here?'

'It's a four-day drive through the mountains and the desert.' Omitting to tell her that a helicopter could make the journey in a matter of hours, Karim watched with satisfaction as something close to horror flickered across her beautiful face. 'Zangrar, as a country, is still comparatively underdeveloped. The terrain is a mixture of sand and rock. When it came to building an international airport, the options were somewhat limited. The fortress city is several days' drive away from here, across harsh desert.'

'No!' Clearly horrified by his announcement, she shook her head vigorously and moistened her lips with the tip of her tongue. 'I studied a map. It looked like a short drive.'

'Distances in the desert are deceptive.'

'I can't do a four-day journey—the desert isn't safe.'

No, it certainly wasn't.

More than content with her reaction, Karim relaxed in his seat. As he'd intended, the princess was clearly afraid of the prospect of a journey through the desert. All he needed to do now was ensure that she spent long enough in those surroundings to convince her that life in Zangrar was *not* going to be to her taste. Once she was exposed to those elements of desert life guaranteed to make a delicately brought-up princess run hard and fast in the direction of the nearest shopping mall, his mission would be virtually complete.

Her eyes were still fixed on his face. 'We have to drive? There is no other way?'

'Four-wheel drive is best.' Pausing, he decided that a little elaboration could only help his cause. 'Camels are equally effective, but obviously not so speedy, and I know that you are desperate to reach the Sultan as fast as possible.'

Apparently missing the irony in his tone, she sank back onto the seat, her breathing rapid as she struggled to control her anxiety.

Karim gave a cynical smile. It wasn't hard to guess the direction of her thoughts. For a girl used to dressing in silk and partying until dawn, a prolonged trip through the desert held little in the way of attractions.

And she was right to be afraid.

By the time she arrived at the Citadel she would, with a little outside assistance, have decided that marriage to the Sultan was not for her. 'Why don't you change your clothes?' She would doubtless select something feminine and unsuitable, and the more unsuitable the dress the more uncomfortable the journey.

And, the more uncomfortable the journey, the faster she would decide to rethink her matrimonial intentions.

Convinced that the success of his mission was already assured, Karim gave a faint smile. 'Welcome to Zangrar, Your Highness,' he drawled softly. 'Welcome to the desert.'

CHAPTER FOUR

WITHOUT a word, Alexa picked up the one small bag that she'd carried on board with her, stood up and moved to the back of the plane.

They were going to travel through the desert and it was going to take *four days*? No. That *couldn't* be right. It was just too dangerous. At any other time she would have been wildly excited at the prospect of exploring the desert, but not right now! Not when so much was at stake.

She didn't know which made her feel more uneasy: the thought of being out in the open where William could intercept them at any time, or the thought of being with Karim.

The memory of waking with her head on his shoulder made her want to curl up and hide with embarrassment.

What was happening to her?

First she'd kissed him—or had he kissed *her*?—and then she'd slept snuggled against him as if they were lovers, not strangers. It didn't make sense. At night she only ever dosed fitfully. She *never* slept. In fact, she'd long since decided that her body had actually forgotten how to sleep properly. In the last sixteen years she hadn't *once* slept for a ten-hour stretch. And yet suddenly she'd done exactly that, and, not only had she slept a deep, dreamless sleep, she'd done it *nestled against Karim*.

It was as if in her sleepy state she'd been somehow aware of his strength and had gravitated towards it.

But that couldn't be the case because she didn't rely on others, did she? Not consciously or subconsciously. No matter how desperate she was, she didn't see Karim as her rescuer. She did things on her own, the way she always had.

She didn't want him here.

Like others before him, he didn't believe that she was in danger, which meant that the danger was suddenly increased, because he would be distracting her when she should be alert.

And he was *extremely* distracting.

Warmth curled inside her as she acknowledged the other reason that she was reluctant to travel with him. It wasn't just that she didn't trust him, was it? It was more than that. She didn't want Karim with her because he made her feel like a woman for the first time in her life. He confused her, with his macho decisiveness and raw sexuality. There was something about the way he looked at her that she found profoundly disturbing. He'd made her feel things she didn't want to feel at a time when the only thing on her mind should have been reaching Zangrar safely.

Alexa groaned aloud with frustration.

She didn't want this now.

Not when she was on her way to her wedding. This was *not* the time to discover that there was actually an intensely passionate side to her nature that had never previously been exposed.

Telling herself that her feelings for the arrogant bodyguard weren't relevant, she dressed swiftly. This wasn't about *her;* her feelings didn't matter and they never had.

All that mattered was reaching the Citadel safely and marrying the Sultan.

She was relying on the Sultan's wealth and influence to help restore Rovina to prosperity.

But if the Sultan refused to help her...

He wouldn't, she told herself firmly as she stuffed her old clothes back into the case. Ruthless he might be, but he was also said to be scrupulously fair. Their fathers had been friends. Surely the Sultan would want to honour the bonds of that friendship?

And as for Karim—well, he was just going to have to learn to follow orders.

Having calmed herself, she walked back to the front of the plane, wearing sand-coloured combat trousers tucked into sturdy desert-boots, and felt a flicker of satisfaction as she saw the surprise in Karim's eyes.

'What's the matter?' She put the case down by her seat. 'You were expecting high heels and a tiara? Don't believe everything you've heard about me, Karim. I knew we had to make at least a short journey through the desert. I've dressed accordingly. What I didn't realise was that it was a four-day journey. I need some time to adjust our travel plans.'

'I have already made the necessary arrangements.' His authoritative tone made her pause.

'*I* make the plans.'

'Not when you are travelling with me, Your Highness. I am your bodyguard. You do as I say at all times. You go where I go and you sleep where I sleep.'

He made it sound impossibly intimate, and suddenly a dangerous heat exploded inside her. 'No way. I'd rather travel on my own.'

'A fool crosses the desert of Zangrar without a guide.'

'A bigger fool trusts another with her life.'

He lifted an eyebrow. 'You doubt my ability to protect you? There is no need. You'll be quite safe.'

Safe.

It was a word that hadn't been part of her vocabulary for sixteen years. The whole concept of 'safe' was a distant fantasy for her. 'How can I be safe when you don't even believe I'm in danger? How can you protect me from a threat you refuse to even acknowledge?'

'The desert is in my blood. If anyone is following us then I will know.'

Alexa stared at him helplessly. She wanted to refuse, but she had to face facts—there was no way she could handle a four-day journey through the desert without expert help. She hadn't planned for that. 'You know the desert well?'

Her reluctantly voiced question drew a faint smile. 'You could drop me blindfold in the middle of it and I would be able to find my way back to the Citadel.'

Arrogant.

That was the other word she'd apply to him. Powerful and *arrogant.*

Alexa looked away from his firm, sensual mouth, trying to think clearly. Relying on anyone else for anything was completely alien to her, but what choice did she have?

She hadn't anticipated a journey of four days.

If she was navigating a complex route, she would never be able to protect herself.

'All right. You do the navigation.' She spoke the words reluctantly, comforting herself with the knowledge that she was still responsible for herself. He was merely providing the transport. 'We travel together.'

But she wasn't going to go where he went, and she *certainly* wasn't going to sleep where he slept.

Two hours later she was beginning to feel relieved that she hadn't attempted the journey alone. The desert was vast, and although the road was clear enough, it was also exposed. There was no way she would have been able to drive and keep watch. There was nowhere to hide and nowhere to run to.

'Can we drive any faster?'

'Not if you wish to reach the Sultan alive with all your limbs still attached to your body.' Karim drove with relaxed ease, sunglasses shielding his eyes from the vicious glare of the sun. 'If your uncle is that desperate to prevent this wedding, then I'm surprised you haven't had doubts yourself.'

'It's the right thing for me.' Uncomfortably aware of his hard, powerful body so close to hers, she kept her eyes forward. It felt bizarre to be discussing her forthcoming wedding while feeling the most intense sexual attraction towards another man. 'You talk a lot for a bodyguard.'

'In our country intelligence is as great an attribute as physical strength, and both are equally necessary.' He gave a faint smile. 'The hunter cannot hunt if he cannot first find his prey, Your Highness.'

Alexa shivered. For the past sixteen years of her life she'd been someone's prey. She'd thought she'd finally escaped, but looking at the dangerous gleam in Karim's dark eyes she suddenly felt the fleeting control she'd had of her life slip through her fingers. She had no doubt that he was now the one in charge, and the thought made her desperately uneasy. Did she want to cross the desert with this man for company? No, she didn't. She didn't want or need other people in her life. She was so much safer alone.

Trying to control her fear, Alexa checked the mirror again for signs of another vehicle, and then tried to relax by studying the scenery.

Before they'd landed in Zangrar she'd seen the desert as nothing more than a land feature that they were going to have to cross. But as Karim had accelerated towards the highway that led through the desert she'd been astounded and then captivated.

Now, as she looked, she saw endless dunes stretching into the distance, the colours myriad shades of burnt orange.

'Like my hair,' she murmured, and Karim glanced towards her. 'What is?'

'The desert. It's the same colour.' For a moment she forgot about William as she gazed out of the window. 'It's astonishing. Fabulous. I never knew that there would be so many colours. I mean, it's just sand, but—' She broke off and shaded her eyes as she squinted towards the top of a steep-sided dune. 'I never thought they'd be that high.'

'Clearly you have never been to the desert before.'

'I've never been *anywhere* before.' Alexa steadied herself as the vehicle bumped over uneven ground. 'This is a better road than I expected.'

'Yes, when you can see it. When the wind blows it lies buried under sand.'

'So how do you find your way when that happens?'

'Modern equipment. And if that lets me down then I rely on experience and more traditional forms of navigation.'

'Such as?'

'The position of the sun, the direction of the wind, the smell of the air.' He shrugged. 'The desert tells you much if you are willing to listen. Why are you asking me, when you apparently intended to travel it yourself with no assistance? Presumably you already possess all these skills?'

'I would have been fine.' Something on the horizon caught her eye. 'There's something moving. I can see something.' Her heart-rate doubled, but Karim didn't slow the vehicle.

'It's a camel train. It's how many people still choose to get around in the desert.'

'Camels?' Alexa stared, fascinated now that she knew it wasn't a threat. 'Can we go closer?'

'You wish to take a closer look at a camel?'

'Is that a problem?'

A look of incredulity crossed his bronzed features. 'No, but it's surprising. A close encounter with a camel wouldn't be high on most women's list of coveted life-experiences.'

'Maybe not. But most women haven't been trapped in one place all their lives. Have you any idea what it's like to see the real thing after staring at a picture?'

'You are telling me that you've never left Rovina?'

Unsettled by her impulsive admission, Alexa clamped her mouth shut. *Why had she told him that?* She knew better than to confide details of her life to anyone.

Ignoring her lack of response, Karim frowned. 'Your uncle is clearly *extremely* protective of you. You should be grateful that he cares so much. Do you not feel that you have betrayed him by running away in the night?'

Protective? 'If you always take things at face value then you're not going to be much use as a bodyguard. Let's just say that my uncle and I seriously disagree about the direction of my future.'

'You are to become Queen in a year. I expect he feels that you should be in the palace, learning everything you can about your new role.'

Alexa leaned her head back against the seat and closed her eyes. She could have told him the truth, of course, but she'd long ago learned the dangers of confiding in *anyone,* so she stayed silent.

But the reminder of Rovina and William had extinguished her innocent enjoyment of the desert, and suddenly Alexa felt sick. There was still so much that could go wrong in the few days before her birthday and the wedding.

She glanced sideways at Karim. *If it came to a fight, would he help her?*

He was certainly capable of it. He was dressed in combat trousers and sturdy boots, and would have looked like a soldier were it not for the dark stubble that hazed his strong jaw after a night of travelling. *Part soldier, part bandit,* she thought dizzily. His hair gleamed blue-black in the harsh desert sunshine, and his bronzed skin betrayed his desert heritage.

He was strikingly handsome and more male than any man she'd met before, his face all hard angles and bold arrogance. He regarded the world with something that came close to disdain, and she knew instinctively that there would be few situations in life that this man wouldn't be able to handle.

Alexa wished desperately that they hadn't shared that explosive kiss. Until that moment she hadn't known how a kiss could feel, and she wished she were still living in blissful ignorance. At least then she wouldn't be using all her energy trying *not* to stare at his mouth.

With the hunger of an addict contemplating the next fix, Alexa's eyes lingered on his powerful shoulders, slid down to his flat, muscular stomach and settled on the hard muscle of his strong thighs. He had the hard physique of a soldier and there was no spare flesh on his lean, powerful frame. The deadly blade of the knife glinted in his belt, and she had no doubt that the gun was also around somewhere close.

'Stop staring at me, Your Highness,' he drawled softly. 'Or is the heat of the desert firing your blood? It has that effect on some people. To be in the desert is to return to life at its most basic and primitive.'

Colour flooded into her cheeks and she looked away immediately, hideously embarrassed that he'd been aware of her scrutiny. 'I wasn't staring.'

'Once you are married to the Sultan you will need to hide the fact that you are attracted to other men.' The vehicle lurched suddenly, and he muttered something under his breath and swung the wheel, skilfully compensating for the deficiencies of the terrain.

Clinging to her seat, Alexa felt her face burn, and suddenly the heat in the car seemed increasingly oppressive. 'I'm not attracted to you.'

'You were gazing at me as you would a lover. The same way you looked at me last night, when you came to my bedroom.'

She'd never had this type of conversation with anyone before, and the breath jammed in her throat. 'I came to your bedroom to find my passport. And I certainly wasn't looking at you as I would a lover. Trust me on that one.'

She'd never had a lover, and after one particularly traumatic experience when she was sixteen she hadn't *wanted* a lover. *Until this moment.*

The thought startled and shocked her, and she rubbed her fingers over her damp forehead, trying to return her mind to its previous state of indifference to romance. The experience of her youth had taught her an important lesson. Once—just once—she'd trusted a man and she'd been paying the price ever since. She hadn't been so much burnt as fried to a crisp. But in a way, that experience had made it easier to do what had to be done. Marriage to the Sultan had somehow seemed less daunting, knowing that love and romance were never going to be an option for her.

Trying to ignore the way Karim made her feel, Alexa stared out of the window, feeling the solid ground of her belief system shifting dangerously beneath her feet. She didn't want to feel like this. *She didn't want to think these things.*

'Try and stay in character, Your Highness,' Karim advised. 'You can't be bold and feisty one minute and embarrassed the next.'

Angered by his remark, Alexa turned. 'That depends on the conversation topic.'

He glanced briefly in her direction, a faint smile touching his hard mouth. 'Thinking about sex is a perfectly natural mind-progression between people of a certain age, wouldn't you agree?'

'No, I wouldn't! And I'm *not* thinking about sex.' But now the word was out there in the open she felt her pelvis burn and her stomach flip. And suddenly she could think of nothing *but* sex. And not sex in the abstract or in general—*sex with Karim.*

With a feeling close to desperation, she felt her eyes stray to his bronzed, capable hands. He handled the vehicle with skill, but the lightness of his touch didn't fool her for a moment. She knew that Karim was in control. *The master.* And then her capricious mind imagined those same confident hands moving over her body, and she suddenly felt as though she'd been seared by the flame of a blow torch. 'Is the air-conditioning working?'

'You grow hot, *habibati?*' His mouth tightened, and it was evident that he didn't welcome the chemistry any more than she did. 'You are worried that you are having such explicit thoughts about one man only a few days before your wedding to another? It's inconvenient, I agree.'

The fact that he'd so clearly guessed her most intimate thoughts left her mortified. 'I'm not thinking about you at all.'

'No?'

'No. And if you think that then you're delusional.'

'I'm honest, Your Highness, but I realize that honesty is not a trait that most women possess, especially when they have their eye on the higher prize.'

'I'm marrying the Sultan in four days.'

'Precisely.' He glanced towards her, but the sunglasses made it impossible for her to read the expression in his eyes. 'You should save those hot, longing looks for your wedding night.'

His words tied her in knots. She didn't want to think about her wedding night. 'I don't want to talk about this any more.'

'Why? It's the future you've chosen. Why wouldn't you want to talk about it?' He turned his attention back to the road. 'I would have thought you would be interested in knowing about the Sultan.'

Her heart was pounding and her mouth was dry. Perhaps talking about the Sultan would return her mind to reality. 'All right. Tell me about him.' It didn't actually matter what they talked about as long as it took her mind off the dangerous chemistry that was pulsing between them.

'He is a typical only child.'

'Overindulged?'

Karim gave a faint smile. 'I was thinking more of the fact that he is a high achiever who is perhaps most at home in his own company.'

'People must fall over themselves to obey his every wish. It must be difficult. He's probably surrounded by people who say what he wants to hear, and he can't really trust any of them because they all have their own agenda.' Her words were greeted by a long silence, and when she glanced towards him she saw that his jaw was tense.

'If you have that degree of insight into the complications of royal life then you are clearly interested in more than shoes and clothes.'

'I've lived in a palace all my life so I know what it's like to be constantly under scrutiny. Everything you do is magnified a hundred times and then reviewed by everyone. I don't suppose it's any different for the Sultan. It's all about manoeuvring and politics. Persuading other people to adopt ideas in a subtle way.'

'The word *subtle* definitely doesn't apply to the Sultan. He gives an order and it is done. That's how things work in Zangrar.'

'No one argues with him?'

'No one would dare. It is not his style to rule by consensus.'

'But you like him?'

Karim frowned. 'I have never before been asked that question.'

'It's a yes-or-no answer.'

He inhaled sharply. 'In that case, it's probably no. I don't think I like him, particularly. In fact, there are occasions when I probably dislike him more than anyone I know. He is infuriatingly autocratic, far too controlling and disturbingly possessive.'

Alexa stared at him, surprised. 'You're very frank.'

'I thought you were looking for the truth.'

'I was, but all the same—aren't you worried that I might tell him what you really think of him?'

Karim laughed. 'No, for two reasons. Firstly, when you are with the Sultan he will not be either wanting or expecting conversation from you. And secondly, the Sultan has absolutely no need or particular desire to be liked. Respect—now, that's a different matter entirely.'

Alexa chose to ignore his oblique reference to sex. 'So you respect him?'

'He and I share a similar vision for Zangrar.'

'And you think he's the man to bring that vision to life?'

'Without a doubt. The Sultan is not a man to entertain the possibility of failure.'

'Well, that's good, then. He wants something badly and he's prepared to go for it.'

'He takes that approach to everything in his life. He decides what is important, and then he pursues that goal relentlessly until it is achieved. He never fails. You might want to remember that.'

'I hope I'll be of use to him.'

'You'll definitely be of use.'

Alexa felt a flicker of disquiet, but chose to ignore the implication behind his words. 'I can give him an impartial opinion.' She knew more about palace politics than most people.

Karim laughed with genuine amusement. 'You think the Sultan will be interested in your opinion? This is Zangrar, Alexa. The Sultan's expectations of your role will not extend beyond the bedroom.'

Suddenly the car seemed like a furnace. 'Don't be ridiculous.'

'I'm being honest. Clearly you haven't thought beyond your wedding.'

Alexa tensed in her seat, knowing that it was true. 'As his wife I can be extremely useful in many ways.'

'There will be only one way that interests the Sultan.' Karim glanced at her briefly, his expression thoughtful. 'But you shouldn't worry about it. As I discovered last night, you are clearly an extremely sexual young woman. I'm sure you'll be able to keep him satisfied, as long as you take plenty of rest in the hours that he is working.'

'Now you really *are* being ridiculous.'

'On the contrary, the Sultan is a man who sets himself a punishing work-agenda. He has little time for relaxation and even less time for physical exercise so these days he tends to combine the two. He has an extremely high sex-drive, but you shouldn't find that a problem. You're clearly a woman with energy and drive of your own. The more I see of you, the more convinced I am that this marriage is to be celebrated by all concerned.'

'The Sultan and I will share a great deal more than sex,' Alexa said stiffly, ignoring the sudden churning of her insides. 'My background is not so dissimilar to his. I'm sure that once I understand him, I'll be able to help in all sorts of ways.'

'The Sultan will not require you to understand him. And he seeks the help of no one. As I said, your role will simply be one of—' he paused as he hunted for the word '—recreation.'

'You can't possibly know that.' Alexa sat back in her seat. 'For a start, he has never even met me. He may not find me attractive.'

'The Sultan does take a great interest in the international press,' Karim said gently. 'Like most people, he is already intimately acquainted with your charms.'

The memory of just how those photographs had been taken made her insides churn with misery. 'Those photographs were taken without my knowledge. I was set up.'

'You weren't really with the man?'

'Yes, I was, but—'

'You don't owe me an explanation. And as for the Sultan…' Karim gave an expressive shrug. 'I have no idea how he feels about it, of course, but it probably isn't a good idea to raise the subject. Obviously he isn't expecting a virgin bride, but that needn't necessarily work to your disadvantage. On the contrary, having an experienced woman in his bed means that he won't feel obliged to curb his appetites. Am I driving fast enough for you?'

His question made her wonder whether he had guessed that she was suddenly wishing they were driving in the opposite direction, and Alexa looked away from him. She didn't want to think about the photographs, she didn't want to think about discussing her past with the Sultan, and she *especially* didn't want to think about being in the Sultan's bed! It just wasn't a thought that had even crossed her mind before now. And then she realized *why* she was feeling so uncomfortable—during all the references to sex with the Sultan, her mind had conjured up disturbingly explicit pictures, and all of them had involved Karim.

The chemistry had been alive from the moment they had met, but it seemed to be growing in intensity with each moment they spent in the desert. Perhaps it was because he seemed so comfortable in these surroundings. Comfortable and confident.

And breathtakingly sexy.

The thought shocked her.

This was *not* the time to be noticing a man.

Alexa kept her eyes forward, reminding herself that marriage to the Sultan could only be a step up from the life she'd had up until now. 'Perhaps the Sultan and I will get on extremely well. Have you known him long?' Glancing towards him, she wondered why the question should make him smile.

'All my life.'

'You were playmates?' She guessed that they were about the same age, so it was the only explanation.

'Of a sort.'

By that he presumably meant that the Sultan was of royal blood whereas he wasn't. 'So you know him well?'

'Too well. I am closely acquainted with all his most irritating personality traits.'

'Such as?'

'The list is endless. He is far too intolerant of the deficiencies of others. Impatient and quick to anger. He's arrogant, and rarely, if ever, believes that anyone else can understand and grasp the subtleties of a situation as well as he can.'

'Perhaps he's right.'

Karim frowned. 'I *wasn't* complimenting him.'

'No, I realize that. But if he's as ferociously clever as they say, then it's entirely possible that no one else *does* grasp the situation as well as he does. Which makes that the truth, rather than arrogance.'

'That's a generous assessment.' He studied an instrument on the control panel and flicked a switch.

'Or maybe simply an alternative assessment. Sometimes the facts don't speak for themselves.' *As she well knew.* 'What else? What matters to him?'

'Honesty and loyalty. Does that worry you, Alexa?'

'No. I appreciate the same qualities.'

'Really? How honest is it to marry a man you don't love?'

'Completely honest, because I'm not pretending to love him.' She glanced towards his arrogant profile, her gaze direct. 'It means that the Sultan and I know where we stand. There are no lies. I think that's a good place to start. I'm confident that we can make this work.'

'And yet you have no idea what the Sultan expects from his wife.'

She didn't care. Once she was safely living in the palace within the high walls of the Citadel, the rest would be irrelevant. They could work it all out, she was sure of it. 'I'll be a good wife.'

'So you're basically happy to do anything at all as long as you have access to his wealth, is that right?'

Not his wealth, no. His protection.

The truth hovered on her lips, but she clamped her mouth shut, bewildered as to why she would even contemplate confiding in this man when she knew the dangers of trusting another person. Hadn't she learned from bitter experience that thoughts were best kept private? 'Does the Sultan have a sense of humour?'

Karim concentrated on the road for a moment. 'In the three years since his father died, there have been many problems in Zangrar, none of which have given much cause for laughter.'

'Disputes over oil and problems with an irrigation project.' Sensing his surprise, she shrugged. 'I can read, Karim. There was a report on the Internet. He takes his responsibilities seriously.' And she'd liked that about him. It had given her hope. *Once she had explained the situation, he would help her with Rovina, surely?*

'The fortunes of Zangrar and the people depend on the Sultan.'

The contrast to William cheered her. 'I'm quite confident that the Sultan and I can have a harmonious marriage.'

'The Sultan isn't a man who could be harmoniously married to anyone.' Karim stopped the vehicle without warning and stared up at the sky.

'What's the matter? Where are we? And where's the road?'

'Underneath the sand. The wind is picking up.' He flicked a switch on the dashboard and several instruments flickered to life. 'The weather is not looking as stable as I would have liked.'

'What are you saying? Is this a sandstorm?' Shielding her eyes from the glare of the sun, she looked at the sky but could see nothing but endless blue, broken by a few wisps of white. 'It looks fine to me.'

'At the moment. Conditions change very rapidly in the desert. We will stop here briefly and rest.'

'Don't stop on my account.' Glancing over her shoulder, she checked that there were no other vehicles in sight. 'I'm quite happy to just push on.'

'It is important to take regular breaks, and crucial to drink.' He opened the door and Alexa felt the sudden rush of heat fill the car.

'I hadn't realized how effective the air-conditioning was. It's hot.'

'It's the desert, Your Highness. Out here temperatures can reach fifty degrees. Without water a human being would not last long. Wait there, I'll come round to you.'

'I don't need help getting out of a car, Karim.' What was he thinking—just because she'd been forced to accept the services of a bodyguard, she was happy to relinquish her independence? No way!

Opening her own door, Alexa was about to jump to the ground when Karim caught her, his strong hands hard on her hips as he pulled her roughly into his arms.

'I told you to *wait*.'

'And I ignored you. I don't know what sort of woman you're used to mixing with, but I'm the sort who can climb down from a car without help.' She wished he'd move his hands from her hips. Caught against his hard, powerful frame, she felt her heart jerk and her body melt. 'What are you doing?'

'Preventing you from killing yourself.' His tone was harsh. 'You *never* step down into the desert without first checking for snakes.'

He was all muscle and masculinity, and her heart was bumping so hard against her chest she could hardly concentrate.

'Snakes?' How was she expected to focus her mind on snakes when all she could think about was *him?*

'This is their home, Your Highness, and during the day they're sleepy and often at their most dangerous. They don't always appreciate being disturbed.'

His gaze flickered over the sand beneath his feet, and then he gently lowered her to the ground, her body sliding down his in a slow, deliberate movement that simply increased her internal agony. Her stomach swooped and she knew that the sudden explosion of heat inside her had nothing to do with the strength of the sun's rays beating down on them.

The sudden harsh intake of his breath indicated that he'd felt it, too.

For a moment they stood there, his fingers biting into her hips, and Alexa couldn't breathe or move, her thoughts and senses smothered by the proximity of his body. She was supposed to be thinking of snakes and the dangers of the desert, but all she could think about was *him* and she felt a flash of panic. *What was it about this man that had such a powerful effect on her?* She never had trouble focusing, never, and yet suddenly...

All she could think about was the kiss they'd shared, and she could see from the slow burn of fire in his eyes that he was suffering a similar torment.

'I'm not that familiar with the rules of the desert.' She forced herself to pull away from him and he released her instantly.

'The Sultan would not forgive me if I failed to protect you.'

'So what do they look like, these snakes?' Her body showed no sign of recovering from the searing heat of the contact. There was a maddening ache between her thighs, and her lips were so dry that she tried to moisten them with her tongue. 'Are they well camouflaged?'

'Extremely well camouflaged. The ability to disguise themselves well is the only thing that stands between them and death in this environment.' His voice was tight and angry, and Alexa knew that he was no more absorbed by the conversation about snakes than she was. In fact, if a snake had picked that moment to come and bite them, there was a strong change that neither would have noticed.

'So now what?' She took another step away from him, hoping that distance might succeed where logic was failing.

'We eat and drink.' Reaching into the car, he pulled out a flask and handed it to her. 'Water. It's another essential part of desert survival. In this heat, you must drink.'

Taking the flask, her fingers brushed against his, and she almost dropped the precious water on the ground. 'This so-called road isn't exactly busy, is it?' Trying to disguise the fact that her hands were shaking, Alexa lifted the flask to her lips and drank. Then she glanced over her shoulder again, as she'd done repeatedly since they'd left the airport. 'Obviously there isn't much traffic between the airport and the Citadel.'

'This is only one of several roads. Are you hungry? Do you want to eat?'

'No, thank you.' Her stomach was churning so badly she knew she wouldn't be able to eat a thing. 'It's hot.'

'Indeed, it is. Even within the stone walls of the fortress the temperatures can reach fifty degrees. Many Western women would find the heat and the dust intolerable. You have led a sheltered life in an air-conditioned palace.'

Sheltered?

He had no idea! 'The heat won't worry me.' But she had a feeling that he wanted it to worry her and for a moment she felt puzzled. Why would the Sultan's bodyguard have an opinion on her impending marriage? Why would he even care?

Karim put the water back in the cooler. 'We should get going. We have a long way to go before darkness.'

'Where are we sleeping tonight?'

'Out in the desert, Alexa. Where else?' He opened the car door for her, a faint smile playing around his firm, sensual mouth. 'You can lie back, look at the stars and dream of the Sultan. Take the opportunity to rest while you can.'

CHAPTER FIVE

THEY reached the tents just as dusk was falling and the setting sun was a deep orange ball in the darkening sky.

Karim was suffering agonies of mental and physical tension. He wasn't sure who had been affected most on the journey. It had been long, trying and *extremely* hot, and he had succeeded in making it hotter still by choosing to talk about topics which would have been best avoided given the intimacy of their current situation.

His plan to plant seeds of doubt in her mind by his descriptions of the Sultan had backfired in the most spectacular way. He'd been in an almost permanent state of arousal since she'd lain underneath him in the bedroom, and his poor choice of conversation topic had merely increased the relentless sexual tension that gripped him. The more he'd talked, the more he'd imagined and the more he'd imagined, the harder it had become to drive.

At one point, he'd been sorely tempted to stop the car and douse himself with the remains of their cold water in a brutal attempt to return his brain to sanity.

But he hadn't taken that option, and to make matters worse— *to raise his temperature still further*—his expansive description of the Sultan's sexual appetites hadn't appeared to worry her that much, which presumably indicated that she believed herself more than capable of matching them.

In the end he'd stopped talking, hoping that a period of re-flection might be sufficient to induce the degree of doubt in her mind that he'd been hoping for. But instead of brooding she'd simply snuggled down and fallen asleep yet again, leav-ing him to cope alone with a rampant attack of unrelieved sexual hunger.

He should have woken her, but he'd taken one look at the blue-black shadows beneath her eyes and the pallor of her skin and found himself unable to rouse her from a sleep she so obvi-ously needed.

Wondering when he'd become such a soft touch, Karim brought the vehicle to a halt outside the tents and glanced at her in exasperation.

All she seemed to do was sleep.

Clearly her hectic lifestyle was catching up with her.

His mouth tightening, he decided that enough was enough. If this woman became Zangrar's queen it would be disastrous, and his absolute priority had to be to prevent it happening. 'Your Highness.' She didn't stir and his tone hardened. *'Alexa.'*

Her eyelids lifted and Karim tumbled headlong into her soft, blue gaze, and suddenly all he wanted to do was spend the fore-seeable future exploring the possibilities of her mouth...

Feeling as though he was losing his grip, he dragged his eyes away from hers and tightened his grip on the wheel. 'We've arrived.'

'Arrived?' Her voice husky, she stretched with feline grace, and then suddenly sat upright sharply. 'Oh my goodness—you should have woken me!'

Wondering whether she was more dangerous awake or asleep, Karim gritted his teeth. 'You were tired. We're spending the night here.'

'You sound cross.' Pushing her hair away from her face, she glanced sleepily out of the window. 'I can't believe I fell asleep again.'

'You've obviously been having too many late nights.'

'I just don't sleep well at home.'

Remembering the picture he'd been shown of her being removed unconscious from a nightclub, Karim was tempted to point out that in order to sleep she had to be in her own bed. Then he remembered that antagonizing her was *not* his objective. 'The heat in the desert can be draining.'

'You should have woken me up and let me drive.'

'There was no need.' Having heard about her accidents, he had no intention of allowing her to drive.

She looked over her shoulder. 'I'm just relieved there's no sign of my uncle.'

'You truly believe that your uncle might follow us?'

'Maybe not in person, but he'll send his men.' Her eyes shifted to his face. 'If he can stop this wedding he will, Karim.'

Suffering from an almost agonizing attack of sexual tension, Karim found himself wishing that her uncle had shown more skill in his persuasion techniques. At least then he wouldn't be facing a night alone in the desert with a female who made him feel uncomfortably out of control.

'We will stay here tonight. It is a regular watering-hole for camel trains. The accommodation will be simple but sufficient for our needs.' And hopefully sufficient to convince her that life in a hot desert-country was not for her. For the sake of his sanity, he hoped she would make the decision sooner rather than later. He could have her back at the airport within a day.

Clearly oblivious to his physical torment, she peered out of the window. 'I didn't think trees grew in the desert.'

'They are date palms. And even in the arid desert, there is water.'

'So, who stays in this place usually?'

'Wandering desert tribes. And tourists wanting to discover the "real" Zangrar.' He opened the door of the vehicle. Immediately a man hurried towards them and fell to his knees. Feeling another surge of tension, Karim spoke softly and watched as the man scrambled to his feet quickly and backed away.

Alexa climbed out of the car and joined him, astonishment on her face as she watched the man. 'Why did he bow? What did you say to him?'

Without missing a beat, Karim slammed the car door shut. 'Unfortunately he guessed that you are the royal princess who is to marry the Sultan. I told him that we don't want your identity revealed.'

'Karim, I look like any other tourist. How could he possibly know who I am?'

'The wedding is an important event of relevance to all the citizens of Zangrar. Everyone in the country is aware of your existence.'

'But if he knows who I am—'

'He will be discreet. Do not worry about him.' Karim pulled her small case out of the back of the vehicle. 'The facilities here are basic, but you should be able to wash in the pool under those trees. Just watch out for the local wildlife.' But if he'd been expecting a show of fear and revulsion at the warning, he was once again disappointed. She simply nodded, apparently more concerned with looking in the direction from which they'd just come.

'By now, my uncle will have realized that we've left. He'll be following us.'

'Such perseverance on his part must make you wonder whether this wedding is wrong for you.' Wondering why she refused to see what was so clear to others, Karim walked towards the tents, gesturing for her to follow him. 'You don't think he has your best interests at heart?'

'No.'

'And yet he has a great deal more life experience than you and knows you well, having cared for you since the death of your parents. It must worry him to see you so set on a marriage that he doesn't believe will make you happy.'

When she didn't answer, Karim sighed. Like most women, she seemed to make a point of rejecting all sensible advice that came her way. It was obvious to him that her uncle understood nothing about the workings of the female mind and had taken entirely the wrong approach. Had he *insisted* on the wedding taking place, there was a strong chance that by now the princess would have decided that marriage to the Sultan was definitely *not* for her.

No matter. If she wasn't willing to accept the decision of others then she'd simply have to make the decision herself.

And he was going to help her.

True, he didn't appear to have made an impact on her yet, but they still had three days of the journey to go through the harshest terrain in Zangrar.

He was confident that by the time they arrived at the Citadel she would have made the decision he wanted her to make.

But, as he urged her inside the simple tent, she turned towards him, her expression suddenly anxious. 'I've got a really bad feeling about this. I think we should just rest for a short time and then carry on with our journey.'

'You are not in charge, Alexa.' He watched as frustration flickered across her beautiful face.

'I could drive while you sleep.'

'That would be beyond foolish. We will both sleep here.'

'And if my uncle is already on our tail?'

Then he could add his persuasion to Karim's. 'I will protect you.' Given that the only threat to her well-being was going to come from him, he wasn't remotely concerned.

'How can you protect me when you don't believe there's a threat? Admit it, you think I'm some sort of hysterical drama queen.'

Karim saw no reason to lie. 'Some women are naturally more nervous than others.'

Alexa hooked her thumbs into the pockets of her trousers. 'Do I strike you as the nervous type? Some women have more *reason* to be nervous than others, Karim. You might want to remember that before you stray too far from your gun.'

'I am prepared to believe that your uncle does not want this marriage to happen, but I am sure he has your best interests at heart. You are the next Queen of Rovina. Clearly he does not think that this is a good time for you to leave the country, but that doesn't mean that he would go to the lengths that you suggest. That would be self-defeating.'

She was silent for a moment, and he sensed that she was on the verge of telling him something important. Then she looked away. 'Fine. If you don't think we should travel at night, then we won't.'

Her sudden compliance filled him with suspicion. 'You are unusually co-operative, Your Highness. If you're thinking of making a dash through the desert on your own, then I ought to warn you that we are sharing a tent tonight. You won't be going anywhere without my knowledge and approval.'

'Sharing a tent? Why would you want to share my tent?'

Karim felt his jaw tense. He didn't want to share her tent, but nor was he so foolish as to let her out of his sight. 'Your safety is my responsibility. My brief is to go wherever you go.'

It was her turn to look suspicious. 'And yet you don't believe that my uncle is a threat.'

No, but it was imperative that he stayed close to her if he was going to ensure that her experience of the desert was not a favourable one. 'I believe that *you* are concerned,' he said smoothly. 'And hopefully my presence should reassure you.'

'Oh.' Her tone suggested that she'd hoped for a different answer. 'Well, that's better than nothing, I suppose. If you insist on sticking to me like glue, then please follow me to the pool. Are you going to swim?'

Karim gritted his teeth. It was hard to say which of the two of them was more tense. 'I will *not* be swimming.' The thought of being semi-naked in the water with this woman sent his body temperature soaring to dangerous levels.

'I thought your brief was to go wherever I go.'

For a moment their eyes held, and awareness pulsed between them like a living force. With ruthless determination, Karim reined in the primitive reaction of his body, struggling to ignore the white-hot flash of lust that engulfed him. 'I will keep watch while you bathe.'

'Fine.'

Angry with himself, Karim paced towards the open flap of the tent and then turned slightly, responding to the tension inside him. *The last thing in the world he wanted to do was watch while she swam naked.* 'You are sure you want to swim? Perhaps you would rather just rest before dinner—sleep again?'

'I just had a sleep. I'm going to bathe. I'm ready when you are.' She flipped open her case and pulled out a small towel. 'I don't have a costume or anything. I'll bathe in my underwear.'

Karim felt beads of sweat sting his brow. He did *not* want to think about her in her underwear.

He didn't want to think of her at all.

Alexa slid under the water, regretting her decision to swim. The pool had seemed to offer an obvious, practical antidote to the heat and dust of the journey. But what she hadn't considered was the impact of being semi-naked with Karim standing so close. She was so hyper-aware of him that, far from feeling cool, she felt feverish and hot.

Not that he was likely to notice. He wasn't even looking at her. Instead he stood with his back to her, his eyes apparently fixed on some far point on the horizon. The late-evening sun shone onto the blade of his knife and it winked and flashed, a deadly reminder that this journey was not a pleasure trip.

But her fear was slightly less acute than usual, and she knew who was responsible for the change in her anxiety levels.

Karim.

Maybe he didn't believe that she was truly in danger, but he was still standing there, wasn't he? He was standing there because of *her,* and for the first time in her life she had a glimpse of what it might be like to not be totally alone.

Alexa studied the width of his shoulders and the power of his body, and wondered for a moment what he would say if she told him the truth about her life.

And then she turned and swam in the opposite direction, horrified that the thought had even entered her head.

That wasn't going to happen.

Confiding in anyone was a mistake, as she'd learned at a pitifully early age when she'd still believed that life was fair and people were good.

And now, *finally,* hope had returned and the only way to give it a chance to blossom into a whole new life was to keep her thoughts to herself and *not* talk. Those skills had been essential to her very survival, and she wasn't about to change that now. It appalled her to think she'd even considered it. Yes, he was watching over her, but only because that was his job. To read sentiment or emotion into his actions would be unforgivably naïve. And she wasn't naïve, was she? Just horribly lonely—but she'd been that way for so long she didn't understand why she would suddenly be reaching out to anyone.

Alexa pulled herself from the water, and then froze as she saw movement out of the corner of her eye. 'Karim—'

'Yes?' The word hissed from his lips, but he didn't turn.

Wondering what possible reason he had to be in such a foul

temper, she kept her eyes fixed on the dust at her feet. 'I think this might be one of those occasions when I need saving. If you're not going to turn around, then I need to borrow your knife. We have a visitor.'

Karim turned swiftly, his hand already closing over the hilt of the dagger. Then he spotted the snake coiled in the shadows of a large boulder and breathed out heavily. 'It's all right. It isn't dangerous.'

'Really? How can you tell?'

'The pattern behind its head.'

Alexa dropped to her knees to take a closer look at the snake, fascinated now that she knew there was no danger. 'I've never seen a real one before. The camouflage is amazing. It's exactly the same colour as the sand. I almost didn't spot it.' She ran a finger over the snake's dry scales and it quickly slithered under the rock, as appalled by the contact as she was intrigued. Rising to her feet, she noticed the incredulity in Karim's eyes. 'What's the matter?'

'It was a snake.'

'Yes.'

'It was a *large* snake.'

Wondering what was responsible for his stunned expression, Alexa shrugged. 'A large snake that wasn't dangerous, according to you.'

'You touched it.'

'Yes—it felt dry. Amazing. Not slimy at all.'

He inhaled sharply. 'Women are not usually overly fond of reptiles.'

'Maybe I've just mixed with more reptiles than most,' Alexa said lightly, glancing towards the rock to see if the snake had reappeared. 'Sorry. Bad joke. If you really want me to have hysterics, then it could probably be arranged.'

'You are unlike any woman I have ever met.'

Unsure whether his observation was a compliment or not, she sighed. 'I'm just not afraid of snakes. Different things frighten different people, I suppose. Do you *want* a hysterical female on your hands? Because if not then I think I'll just get dressed. I feel a bit vulnerable standing here half-naked.'

His burning gaze slid from her face to her breasts, and immediately she wished she hadn't drawn attention to her state of undress. His eyes lingered before moving down over her waist to her skimpy pants. Aware that her flimsy wet underwear provided her with no cover whatsoever, Alexa turned quickly and pulled on her cargo trousers, ignoring the fact that the material clung to her still-damp body.

A shout from the camp disturbed them.

'People are coming.' Karim thrust her shirt towards her. 'Get dressed.'

'I'm doing my best, believe me.' Fumbling with the buttons, her cheeks blazing, Alexa finally secured her shirt. The dip in the water had cooled her, but now she felt uncomfortably hot again and knew that it was nothing to do with the desert heat and everything to do with Karim. He was standing so close that they were almost touching, and she knew that even if they'd been traversing the Arctic Circle she would still have felt hot. All she could think about was her body—*his body*.

What was it about him?

Or was it her? Helpless to understand what was going on, she almost groaned in despair. Had she been locked up in one place for too long? Had her loneliness made her desperate? Had she developed some sort of fixation on her bodyguard because he was offering her protection? Some women did that, she knew. They were attracted to strong, powerful men. But she wasn't that sort of woman. Since the death of her father, she hadn't had a man's protection, and she no longer expected or needed it. And she wasn't interested in any other sort of relationship, either.

Yes, she was marrying the Sultan, but only because that was what she had to do.

She owed it to the people of Rovina, many of whom she knew had abandoned hope when her uncle had become the Regent.

Suddenly Alexa felt a flicker of disquiet as the reality of her situation slammed home. Duty or not, she *was* going to be marrying a man she'd never met, and that had suddenly taken on a new significance.

And she knew why.

Her gaze flickered to Karim. Sex suddenly seemed significant because for the first time in her life she was aware of herself as a woman. Karim had awakened her sexuality, feelings that she hadn't known existed.

Her fingers shook as they fumbled with the last of her buttons. This was *not* the time to discover that she had a whole side to herself that she'd never imagined was there. She needed to focus on getting safely to the Citadel and marrying the Sultan, and it didn't matter if he had four heads and no personality—she would still be marrying him.

She had to.

Her life depended on it.

The future of Rovina depended on it.

'I will escort you back to the tent. There will be time to rest before we eat.' His tone icy-cold and discouraging, Karim led her back along the sandy path that led from the oasis through the trees. 'You should rest now. I'll call you when it's time to eat.'

'I don't need to sleep.' How could she sleep when she was her own bodyguard? She needed to keep watch.

'Then rest, at least.' Karim frowned, as if her response had annoyed him. 'I'll be just outside the tent.'

She made no sense whatsoever.

And his reaction to her made even less sense. At one point

he'd been on the verge of stripping off and joining her in the pool, and as if that hadn't been surprising enough he'd then found himself regretting the fact that he was no longer able to follow such impulses.

Karim frowned. These days his mind rarely strayed from duty and responsibility, and yet there had been moments on the journey when…

He cut the thought off before it could develop and fixed his eyes on the road that stretched into the distance, reminding himself that his objective was to show the princess the horrors of the desert.

But so far he wasn't doing very well, was he?

The unexpected appearance of the snake had been particularly timely, but her reaction had been especially astonishing. Once she'd ascertained that it wasn't poisonous, she'd shown interest rather than either the fear or revulsion that he'd anticipated and hoped for.

Off hand, he couldn't think of a single woman of his acquaintance who would have welcomed the opportunity to take a closer look at a snake, and certainly none who would have chosen to examine it at close quarters.

She'd touched it. She'd bent and stroked it as if it had been a domestic pet, and there had been something about that gentle, almost seductive touch that had sent his pulse-rate soaring into the stratosphere.

Wondering what it was going to take to unnerve her, Karim ran a hand over his face, reflecting on the irony of the situation. For the first time in his life he'd met a woman who seemed perfectly at home in these harsh surroundings. How many times in the past had he dreamed about finding a woman who shared his love of Zangrar?

Staring into the desert, he found himself wondering what it would have been like to meet her under different circumstances, and then he closed his eyes briefly, frustrated by his inability to control his own libido around a woman who possessed virtually no admirable qualities.

Yes, her fascination with the desert was surprising, and might actually have been gratifying in different circumstances—but not *these* circumstances.

The fact that she seemed comfortable with the heat, the dust and the wildlife was not enough to make 'the rebel princess' a suitable wife.

Glancing over his shoulder towards the sealed tent, he wondered what she doing now.

Was she asleep yet again?

Or was she lying on the bed dreaming of the riches that awaited her in Zangrar?

Refreshed after her swim and dressed in a pale blue linen dress that fell to her ankles, Alexa wandered out of the tent and bumped straight into Karim.

Disturbed by how good it felt to know he was there, she just stood there, and eventually he broke the tense silence.

'Food will be served by the fire. It keeps the wildlife at bay.' His harsh tone suggested that he wasn't similarly pleased to see her, and she was appalled by how much that knowledge disappointed her.

'I quite like the wildlife. It's very interesting. What sort are we talking about this time?'

His gaze flickered to her clothes and down to her strappy sandals. 'The sort that would grow excited when faced by a pair of bare feet.'

'Are you trying to frighten me, Karim? All you seem to do is tell me about the dangers of the desert.'

'Clearly you're *not* frightened.'

'I love it.' She looked around her. 'I love everything about it. The colours, the solitude, the sheer enormity of the place, reminding you how small and insignificant you are—' She broke off and gave a tiny shrug, embarrassed by her outburst. 'I have never left Rovina before. I haven't been in possession of my passport since I was eight years old.'

'That was when your parents were killed?'

It was a conversation topic that had never come up, and for a horrifying moment her brain was filled with images that paralyzed her.

'Alexa?'

Hearing Karim's voice, she pushed through the dark, terrifying clouds. 'Yes.' Somehow she persuaded her voice to work. 'My uncle didn't want me going anywhere.'

'As your guardian, he clearly takes his responsibilities very seriously.'

Reminded of the reality of her life, Alexa stood still. 'What time will we set off in the morning?'

'Early.' Karim gestured towards the rug that had been placed next to the fire. 'Sit. You must be hungry'

'Not really. I just want to finish the journey.'

'I guarantee your safety, Alexa. I just hope that marriage to the Sultan is all that you are hoping for.'

In desperate need of distraction, she concentrated instead on the robed man who was placing various dishes on the rug between them. 'Let's forget about the Sultan for five minutes. Tell me about yourself. You grew up in the Citadel? Has your family always worked for the Sultan?'

'We have always been close to the Sultan, yes.' He listened while the man spoke to him in a low voice, and then shook his head and dismissed him with a wave of his hand.

Alexa watched as the man melted away. 'Is there a problem?'

'He wanted to know whether he should fetch you a knife and fork. I told him that you want the full desert-experience. That's right, isn't it, Your Highness? That is what you've signed up for, after all.'

'Obviously I'm eager to learn as much as possible,' she said honestly. 'Would the Sultan stay in a desert camp like this one?'

'Occasionally. Sometimes the accommodation would be

much more basic, usually it would be more luxurious. It really depends on the purpose of the trip.'

'And you go with him?'

'Always.'

'He must be missing you.' Alexa took the cup that was handed to her and drank thirstily. 'It's good. What is it?'

Karim lay sprawled on the rug, his dark eyes lazily amused. 'Camel's milk.'

'Really? It's delicious.' She drank again and saw his surprise. 'What? It's rude to stare, Karim.'

'You are used to drinking fine wines from cut glass. Camel's milk from an earthenware cup must be an entirely new experience.'

'But not all new experiences are bad ones.' She finished her drink and selected some food from the dishes in front of her, following Karim's lead and eating with her fingers. 'Did you spend much time in the desert when you were young?'

'Yes. My family's roots are in the desert, and many of our people still lead nomadic lives. It's essential to understand the particular hardships and problems that they face.'

'So that you can understand the Sultan's work, you mean? Or so that you can protect him more effectively?'

'Both.'

'And now you live in the Citadel itself? In the palace?'

'Of course. I go where the Sultan goes.'

'Then I'll be seeing a lot of you once I'm married.'

Karim stared into the fire, and when he finally lifted his gaze to hers there was a mockery in his eyes that she didn't understand. 'If you marry the Sultan, then you will certainly see a great deal of me.'

Alexa felt her heart stumble. The thought of seeing Karim every day was unsettling to say the least. 'Why do you say *if*?'

The reflection of the fire flickered in his liquid dark eyes. 'The Citadel is a fortress, Alexa, not a shopping mall. If the Sultan so wishes, he can keep you inside his palace and not allow you to see the light of day. Is that truly a life that can make you happy?'

Alexa smiled at the thought. Life in a fortress. *With her uncle on the outside.* 'It's what I want.'

'You *want* to be closeted behind high stone-walls with a man you have never even met? It seems a strange choice.'

'That's because you know nothing about my life.'

'Then tell me.' He leaned towards her, his gaze compelling and his voice surprisingly gentle. 'Tell me about your life, Alexa. What is it that makes this match so appealing? We are alone, now, just the two of us. Talk to me.'

Alexa stared at him. She'd lived her entire life alone, devoid of love and friendship, and the sudden flicker of warmth in his eyes was enough to draw her out in much the same way as a starving animal would tiptoe towards the promise of a morsel of food.

'I've never told anyone.'

'Then it is time to confide in someone,' he urged. 'Because such introverted behaviour is *not* natural for a woman.'

Most women hadn't lived her life.

The past oozed into her brain like a deadly cloud, souring the atmosphere, and she scrambled to her feet quickly. She was doing it again! The urge to confide in him was becoming stronger and stronger despite the fact that she knew the dangers of speaking to the wrong person. 'The meal was lovely. Please thank them for me. If we have an early start, then I think it's best if I go to bed now.'

CHAPTER SIX

SHE'D been on the verge of telling him something. The question was, *what?*

And why was he so interested?

Simmering with frustration at her abrupt departure, Karim stood outside the tent, giving her time to prepare herself for bed before joining her. What confession had been clinging to her lips?

Regret for the life she'd led?

Second thoughts about marrying a man just for status and money?

Wondering if her conscience was keeping her awake, he pushed aside the flap of the tent and strode inside.

One glance told him that she was already asleep, apparently oblivious to the hard, simple bed, the spartan surroundings or the nagging of her conscience.

Her luxurious red-gold hair was spread haphazardly over the pillow like sand blown by the wind, and her mouth was the colour of ripe strawberries. *Strawberries just waiting to be devoured.*

Even in the depth of sleep she looked like every man's hottest fantasy, and Karim experienced a monumental surge of desire as he stood watching her. The ache in his loins grew to agonizing levels, and he uttered a soft curse and strode to the far side of the room, vowing to stay as far away from her as possible.

Why had he imposed this ridiculous rule that she was to stay by his side for the entire journey? Just who was suffering most?

He lay down and waited for sleep to claim him, but it was asking the impossible, and he was still staring grimly upwards when the princess gave a frightened moan.

Karim was on his feet with the speed and grace of a panther, the hilt of the knife in his hand as he prepared to defend her.

'Alexa?' The fading light of the hurricane lamp was enough to show him that no one had entered the tent without his knowledge, which meant that her distress was caused by something different.

Spider? Scorpion?

His senses on alert, Karim prowled silently over to the large bed and stared down at the princess who was now sprawled on her back, one arm flung upwards, her cheeks flushed.

Evidently she was still asleep, which meant that her distress was caused by nothing more than a bad dream. So perhaps her conscience was pricking her, after all.

Slowly he returned the knife to his belt, his attention held by the expanse of creamy bare shoulder revealed by crumpled bedsheet. Forcing his gaze upwards, he noticed the faint sheen of sweat on her brow, and then she cried out again and this time he saw the trickle of tears on her cheeks.

Shocked by the sight of those tears, Karim froze.

Completely out of his comfort zone, he then took an involuntary step backwards, retreating from such a visible display of emotion as he would a wild beast.

In fact, he would have been far more comfortable rescuing her from the jaws of a lethal predator. He *hated* tears. In early childhood he'd been given endless opportunity to observe the many uses of female tears, but even he had never before witnessed a woman cry in her sleep.

Reluctantly, he was forced to acknowledge that these were

real emotions, not those constructed specifically to extract something from a man, and he stood frozen with indecision as those silent tears ripped holes through his iron-clad defences in a way that no physical weapon would have done. Suddenly he felt raw and exposed as long-forgotten images settled over his brain like a toxic cloud.

His natural aversion to emotional scenes stifled his ability to think clearly, and he stood paralyzed. What was he supposed to do? He knew *nothing* about dealing with a woman whose tears were genuine.

And then he realised that he didn't have to do anything.

She was asleep, wasn't she?

No action was required on his part.

Relieved to have reached that conclusion, Karim was about to return to his bed when she gave another cry, and this time the sound was so tortured that he sat down next to her.

What was he doing?

What did he know about comforting anyone? It was far more usual for him to be the cause of female tears.

Deciding that by far the simplest and safest solution would be to wake her up so that she could solve the problem herself, he reached out a hand and gave her shoulder a firm shake.

She awoke instantly with a horrified gasp, her eyes wide and terrified.

'Go away!' She sat bolt upright, her expression stricken. 'Don't *touch* me!' Her fist powered into his stomach with surprising force, and the breath hissed through his teeth as pain radiated across his abdomen.

'It's me,' he grunted, closing his fingers over her fist before she could do any more damage, 'Karim. You were dreaming.'

As he waited for the blankness in her eyes to fade and the pain in his muscles to settle, he reflected on the fact that the princess hadn't been exaggerating her claim that she could manage perfectly well without a bodyguard. No one could have described her as defenceless.

So how could a woman who could deliver a punch like that appear vulnerable?

Her breathing was rapid and she gave a little shake of her head, her cheeks still wet with tears. 'Sorry. I—I had a dream.'

'Yes.' Relieved that the problem appeared to be solved, Karim released her hand and started to stand up, but she grabbed his arm.

'Wait a minute. Don't go. Please don't leave me.'

Her request was so unexpected that he simply stared at her. *What did she expect him to do?* 'You're awake now.'

'It's all still in my head. It was so clear…' Her fingers tightened on his arm and he had little choice but to sit down again.

'Think about something else,' he advised swiftly, and she made a sound that was somewhere between a sob and a laugh, fully awake now.

'Sorry. This isn't what you signed up for, is it? Go back to bed, I'll be fine.' With obvious reluctance, she released her desperate grip on his arm and bent her knees up to her chest, cuddling them like a child. 'I'm sorry if I disturbed you.' She was shaking so badly that Karim could feel the movement on the mattress, and he gave an impatient sigh.

'It was just a dream, Alexa.'

'Yes.' Her teeth were chattering and she buried her head in her arms. 'Go back to bed.'

He should have done exactly that, but somehow he couldn't bring himself to leave her, and that impulse puzzled and exasperated him. 'What was the dream about?'

Her head lifted and she looked at him, tears spilling out of her eyes and onto her cheeks. She made no sound, but simply blinked a few times and then brushed her tears away impatiently. 'It doesn't matter.'

'You need to go back to sleep,' he said roughly. 'Whatever it was all about, the memory will have gone in the morning.'

'Not all memories are so easily erased.' She spoke softly, as if afraid that to raise her voice might make those memories still more vivid. 'I thought this would be a fresh start. I thought that I could finally leave it all behind. But it comes with you, doesn't it? It follows you everywhere, because it's been there for so long, it's part of who you are.'

Was she talking to herself or to him?

Was she seriously expecting some sort of response?

Karim had no idea what she was talking about, but it sounded disturbingly like the sort of touchy-feely conversation that a woman ought to have with another woman. '*What* follows you?

'The past. It's always there. You can never shake it off.'

Confronted with a more clearly defined problem to deal with, Karim relaxed slightly. It was obvious that she regretted the things she'd done in her past, and that was hardly surprising, given just how wild her behaviour had been. Evidently her impending marriage to the Sultan had made her wish that she'd behaved with a little more restraint in her youth, which meant that it *was* her conscience that was disturbing her sleep.

'The past is the past.' Wishing that she'd stop shaking, he kept his words blunt. 'There is never any point in looking back. It's over and done with.'

'That isn't true. Don't *you* ever look back?'

'No,' Karim said shortly. 'The past is over. The future is the only thing that matters. And your future requires us to leave at dawn. If you don't get some sleep soon you'll be too tired to travel.'

'I don't want to go back to sleep. Can we leave now? I'm scared, Karim.'

'We're not leaving. Lie down.'

For once, she didn't argue. Like a child obeying a parent, she lay down, and Karim stared at her shivering, half-naked form with exasperation. Wasn't she going to pull the covers up?

After a moment's hesitation he reached out and tugged the sheet up over her shoulders, covering her body and at the same time pondering on the entirely new experience of tucking a beautiful woman into a bed that he wasn't sleeping in. As he rose to his feet her hand shot out and her slim fingers gripped his arm again.

'Will you stay? Just for a moment.'

Her fingers tightened on his arm and he covered them with his own. Her slender fingers were freezing cold, and he rubbed his hand over hers and then realized what he was doing and released her instantly. 'You'll be fine now.'

What was he doing?

What instinct had driven him to offer comfort when he was so inexperienced in that particular skill?

'*Please* stay with me. Just for a minute.'

For what purpose? What did she want from him? His eyes raked over her shivering body, but there was nothing in the least seductive about the way she lay. She looked fragile and vulnerable as she huddled under the sheets, as if she were trying to make herself as small and insignificant as possible.

'*What* are you afraid of?' Irritated with himself for responding to her, his voice was rougher than he'd intended. 'Tell me.'

'Why—so that you can take out your gun and shoot it?' She gave a shaky laugh, released his arm and curled up into a ball. 'There are some things that even a bodyguard can't protect you from, and this is one of them. You're right. You can't help me, Karim. Go back to bed. I'm sorry I disturbed you.'

He had her permission to leave.

So why was he still standing there?

Something about her weary dismissal made it impossible for him to walk away, and the urge to help and protect her was so shockingly powerful that he almost laughed at himself. *So he wasn't entirely immune, then.* Just like his father before him, he was a man capable of being manipulated by a woman's tears.

'There is nothing to be afraid of.' He was impatient with himself, not her, but he saw her withdraw.

'I'm fine, Karim. Go to bed.'

Frustrated by his inability to do exactly that, Karim frowned down at her, studying the dark shadows under her eyes and the almost translucent skin over delicate bones. *She didn't look fine.* She looked like a woman who was hunted by demons. And she was a woman of contrasts—strong and feisty one minute, vulnerable the next. *How had a woman who looked as though a gust of wind could snap her in two, shown such resilience in the desert?* 'Was your dream to do with your uncle?'

'Can we talk about something else? Anything.' Sounding more like a nervous child than a grown woman, she huddled under the covers. 'It would help a lot if you could just talk about something normal for a moment. Tell me about your family.'

'My family is *not* normal,' Karim said dryly. 'I suggest you pick a different topic.'

'*You* pick a topic.'

'I'm not good at small talk.'

'Then it will be useful to practice. Come on, Karim. Talk to me.'

Talk? Telling himself that the sooner she settled down the sooner they'd both get some sleep, Karim sighed and rubbed his fingers over his temple. 'Have you ever heard of dune driving? Because the next stretch of our journey has some of the best dune driving in Zangrar. Steep dunes, spectacular views, exciting drops. It's the best adrenaline rush in this part of the world—' he broke off, surprised at himself. Why had he picked that particular topic? What was it about Alexa that made him remember the heady days when pleasure had come before responsibility?

'Don't stop,' she murmured. 'I want to hear more. You did it when you were young?'

'As soon as I could drive.'

'And did the Sultan go with you?'

Karim stilled. '*Always* you ask about the Sultan.'

'I'm trying to build up a picture.'

'Yes,' Karim said finally. 'Before life became too serious to allow such frivolities, the Sultan had a passion for dune driving.'

'What does it involve?'

'Driving up the side of a dune and plunging over the top. A bit like a roller coaster, only less predictable and more hair-raising. And a great deal more uncomfortable if you topple the vehicle.'

'Did you?'

'A few times.' Karim started to smile and then stopped himself, remembering that this was supposed to be distraction therapy, not a trip down memory lane.

'It sounds dangerous.' Her voice was sleepy. 'I'm surprised the Sultan was allowed to do that if he was the heir to the throne. Wasn't he surrounded by people telling him what to do?'

'He was sent to boarding school at the age of seven, and from there went straight into the army. The time he spent in Zangrar was very precious because no one really bothered with him.'

It was a long time before she spoke. 'That's a very young age to leave your parents.'

'It is the custom.'

'I wouldn't do that with my children. I'd keep them close. Didn't the Sultan's mother object to him being sent away? Or wasn't she given any choice?'

Increasingly discomforted by the direction of the conversation, Karim made a mental note *never* to wake a distressed woman from sleep again. Suddenly the atmosphere in the tent seemed dangerously intimate and filled with shadows of the past that her words had inadvertently released. 'The Sultan's mother died when he was little more than a toddler. He was sent away by his stepmother.'

'Oh. That's terrible,' she breathed softly. 'Then it's no wonder that he isn't interested in emotional relationships, is it? He's probably had no experience of love.'

'I thought you didn't believe in love.'

'I didn't say that.' She smothered a yawn and her eyes drifted shut, her thick, dark lashes forming two perfect crescents on her pale cheeks. 'I said that *this* marriage isn't about love. That doesn't mean I don't think love exists. Actually, I do believe that love exists. For the lucky few. It's finding it that's the problem.'

Deciding that the conversation had progressed far beyond his comfort zone, Karim rose to his feet. 'You should rest.'

She didn't even answer and he realized that she was already asleep, her breathing even and peaceful, the tears on her cheeks now dry.

Karim stared down at her with exasperation and then strode back to his corner of the tent, aware that, while she'd drifted back into the welcome oblivion of sleep, he now had to deal with all the uncomfortable and unfamiliar emotions that their conversation had aroused.

And one thing he knew for sure—sleep would be a long time in coming.

Alexa woke to find herself alone in the tent.

Then she heard Karim's voice just outside and knew that he hadn't gone far. Not that she would have blamed him if he had. After being subjected to the torrent of her emotions the night before, a man like Karim must be stifling the urge to sprint fast in the opposite direction.

She closed her eyes, feeling washed out and weedy. It was a recurring nightmare and it always had the same effect on her.

But it was the first time that she'd shared the experience with anyone. And not just anyone, but a man who epitomized everything it meant to be tough and strong. *A man, to whom the mere concept of being frightened by something so intangible as a dream, must have been unfathomable.*

Alexa covered her face with her hands and gave a groan of embarrassment.

What must he have thought? Even in the depths of her distress, she'd sensed his discomfort. The only reason he'd remained seated on the bed was because she'd gripped his arm and begged him not to leave her.

But he hadn't left her, had he?

Despite being dramatically out of his comfort zone, he'd stayed by her side until she'd fallen asleep. And, because she knew that it hadn't been an easy thing for him to do, it somehow made the gesture all the more touching. He'd stayed, and that was what mattered. Clearly an upset woman wasn't his favourite challenge, but he'd remained by her side until she'd fallen asleep.

No one had ever done that for her before. Not one person.

Pondering on that thought, Alexa slid out of bed, dressed swiftly in her trousers and combat boots, twisted her long hair into a coil and secured it on top of her head. Dressed, she felt more in control. Or did she feel more in control because she'd shared her darkest moment with Karim?

For the first time in her life, she hadn't felt alone.

Feeling pathetically grateful towards him, Alexa left the tent and was immediately confronted by his powerful shoulders and lean, long legs. He was in conversation with several men from the camp, but he turned as he heard her emerge from the tent. Their eyes met and held.

He said nothing, and yet the moment felt intensely personal— a silent acknowledgement of a secret shared. Then he gave a brief nod and Alexa felt her insides tumble. Suddenly she felt ridiculously nervous and had absolutely no idea why.

'Good morning.'

He dismissed the man he was talking to with an abrupt wave of his hand. 'You are feeling all right?'

She dug her hands in her pockets. How was she supposed to reply to that? No, she wasn't feeling all right. Suddenly she felt as vulnerable as she'd felt when she was eight years old, clinging to the desperate hope that someone, somewhere would care for her and take the pain away if only she could find them.

But at least at the age of eight, she'd had childhood on her side as a decent excuse for such foolish fantasies.

What excuse was she using now?

Her eyes slid to Karim.

What was it about the dark and the dreams that had turned her into a child again? Why was she longing to trust him, when she'd long since discovered that the only person she could trust was herself?

Was it because, for the first time in sixteen years, she'd shared her past? She hadn't had to cope with it alone, and that had felt good. And, now that she'd experienced the warmth of human comfort, it no longer seemed easy to shut her emotions away. She wanted more, and the power of that need terrified her more than the nightmare itself.

She wanted to feel his touch again. She wanted to reach out and touch *him*.

But that wasn't allowed, was it? Although his gaze held hers, he held himself slightly apart—distant and unapproachable, as if warning her that the intimacy that they'd shared during the hours of darkness could not be extended into the daylight.

She was alone again.

A little masculine comfort in the darkness of the night had changed nothing, except perhaps to make everything seem just that little bit worse. Because that taste of human comfort had left her thirsty for so much more.

'I'm fine, Karim.' Too confused about her own feelings to hold his gaze a moment longer, she glanced away. 'I'm sorry about last night. Not your favourite scenario, I'm sure.'

He didn't reply, and she wished she'd had the sense not to raise the subject. Even though they weren't touching she could feel the tension in his powerful frame, and sensed that he had every intention of avoiding any reference to the conversation that they'd had in the dark recesses of the night. She sucked in a breath. 'Anyway, I just wanted to say thank you. You were— kind.' It seemed a completely inappropriate word for this man, who was the complete antithesis of the word *kind,* and perhaps he thought so, too, because his dark eyes narrowed slightly as he studied her face in brooding silence.

Finally he spoke. 'No apology is needed. You had a long and tiring day. Enough to trigger bad dreams in the most robust personality.'

'Yes.' There was no need to tell him that the dreams had nothing to do with the day they'd had and everything to do with her dark and tangled past. He didn't need to hear that. *He didn't want to hear it.* The loneliness of her situation rose up inside her and threatened to swallow her whole.

Karim took a step backwards, his tone cool and lacking in encouragement. 'We should leave. Eat something.' He waved a hand towards a rug that had been spread out in front of the tent. 'I'll meet you by the car when you're ready.'

Alexa watched him stride off and dropped onto her knees on the rug, not at all feeling like eating. She nibbled a few dates and some pita bread and took a few sips of water, before returning to the tent to pack her things. *Keep moving forward. Never look back.*

Karim was already loading the four-wheel drive. 'Are you ready?'

'Yes.' She handed him her small case and he stowed it in the back. 'How far are we going today?'

'We should reach the next oasis. It's much bigger than this place. More of a tourist resort. From there it is less than two days' drive to the Citadel. You should be in plenty of time for your wedding.'

'Wedding.' Alexa stared at him and he lifted an eyebrow.

'You'd forgotten your wedding?'

'Don't be ridiculous. Of course not.' But she had. Just briefly, her life had condensed itself down to this one single moment, and the only man in her mind was him. But now she was duly reminded that there was so much at stake. As if remembering that fact, she glanced once over her shoulder and then slid into the car, trying to ignore Karim in the seat next to her.

Strong, she thought wistfully. During the night it had been his strength that had comforted her. And she had to remind herself that there had been nothing personal in the gesture.

'So—tell me about this dune driving.' Trying to distract herself, she covered her eyes with her dark glasses and stared out of the window at the towering dunes that surrounded them. 'They look pretty high. You drive right to the top?'

'And down the other side and then back up to the top again.'

'Sounds fun. Can we do it?'

He glanced towards her, dark eyes incredulous. 'You want to drive to the top of a dune?'

'I thought we could both do with a little light relief.'

'I haven't done it since I was in the army.'

'So what's that supposed to mean—are you too old to have fun?' A devil inside her made her tease him. Or perhaps she was just overcompensating for the misery she felt. 'Or have you lost your nerve since then, Karim?'

'It is *your* nerve that concerns me. You may be a rebel, but I don't think you're brave.'

Aware that he was referring to the tears she'd shed the night before, she drew in a deep breath. 'My nerve is intact. I thought you wanted to show me the desert. So take me to the top of a dune and show me your desert, Karim.'

For a moment she thought he was going to refuse. Then he turned towards her, his dark eyes gleaming with challenge. 'Do you like roller coasters?'

Alexa sensed a change in him. Suddenly he seemed lighter—*less intimidating*—and the tantalizing glimpse of this hidden part of him intrigued her. 'I've never been on a roller coaster. Try me.'

'You promise not to scream like a girl?' A faint smile tugged at the corners of his normally serious mouth, and that smile was so surprising that she felt her stomach flip.

'I promise not to scream like a girl. Go for it. Rediscover your reckless youth.'

'All right. Hold on.' Without giving her a chance to change her mind, he turned the wheel, flattened the accelerator and the vehicle shot straight to the top of the dune.

The sudden rush of speed made her wish she hadn't been quite so rash, and if she could have changed her mind in that split second then she would have done.

Why, oh, why, had she encouraged him to behave like an irresponsible teenager?

As they roared up the side of the steep dune she clutched her seat and cast a look at his profile—and saw not a teenager, but a man.

His eyes were fixed ahead in total concentration, his hands moving instinctively over the controls as he demanded the utmost from the vehicle. And his cool confidence soothed her anxiety and she found herself relaxing, and then gasping with amazement as they crested the dune and she saw more dunes stretching out ahead of them like an exotic, fiery labyrinth.

'Oh, it's beautiful,' she breathed. 'So beautiful. Like another world.'

For a moment they were poised on the top of that world, and

then Karim threw her a slow, wicked smile and hit the accelerator with his foot. The vehicle plunged nose-first down the vertiginous drop on the other side, forcing Alexa to throw out a hand and steady herself against the dashboard.

It was so thrillingly terrifying that at first she couldn't catch her breath. Resisting the temptation to cover her eyes, she braced herself for the moment when the vehicle would topple over and land upside down at the foot of the dune, but it didn't happen. Instead they descended the dune in a smooth rush, Karim handling the wheel so skilfully that Alexa laughed with exhilaration.

They reached the bottom and he jerked on the handbrake.

She gulped in some much-needed air and then turned to look at him, unsure as to exactly what was responsible for her churning stomach: terror or the impact of the devastating smile he'd given her. 'Is this what they teach you in the army?'

'Desert survival.' Still smiling, he released the handbrake and drove back towards the road. 'You're a very surprising woman, do you know that?'

'Because I didn't scream like a girl? I didn't have the breath to scream.'

'Because you're not afraid of any of the things I would expect you to be afraid of. You shrug off the heat, you stroke a snake and you laugh at dune driving—but you hate locked doors, cry in your sleep and you run from a man who has no reason to chase you.'

Her smile faltered. 'Well, fear is a funny thing, isn't it? It's different things for different people.' Dark clouds swirled around her brain like a malevolent stalker ready to snuff out her brief flirtation with happiness. 'Can I have a go behind the wheel?'

'You *have* to be joking.'

His reaction made her laugh. 'So is this *your* fear, Karim? A woman behind the wheel?'

'Driving in the desert is very different to driving on tarmac. The sand is constantly shifting. It isn't as easy as it looks.'

'It doesn't look easy at all. But it looks fun. That's why I want to try it.' Alexa couldn't remember a time when she'd laughed like that, and suddenly she was desperate to recapture the moment. 'Can I?'

'You forget that I've already experienced your driving once. Even without the presence of a sand dune, it was scary.'

'That's not fair. I was afraid we were being followed.'

'You drove like a madwoman,' Karim muttered, adjusting several controls on the dashboard and steering the vehicle back onto the sandy road that cut between the undulating dunes. 'If that is how you drive, then it is no wonder that you have had accidents.'

The feeling of happiness left her as abruptly as it had arrived. 'My accidents had absolutely nothing to do with my driving.'

'You are saying that the tree jumped out and banged into your car?'

'No. I—' *Oh what was the point?* His job was simply to escort her safely to the Citadel, not provide her with emotional support. She didn't need emotional support. 'Accidents happen, Karim.'

He watched her for a moment, his gaze disturbingly acute. '*Not* when I am your bodyguard.' He sounded so confident that for a moment she wanted to believe him. It would have been so tempting to just relax and let someone else take the pressure for a change.

But she knew she couldn't do that.

An unexpected moment of lighthearted fun didn't change the facts. Her life was in danger, and she wouldn't be safe until they were inside the high stone-walls of the Citadel.

CHAPTER SEVEN

THEY arrived at the oasis as dusk was falling.

Alexa watched as Karim avoided the busy tourist hub and drove the vehicle to an elaborately tented area slightly set apart. 'They call this the Royal Suite. It has been set aside for our use. It's more private than the other accommodation.'

'I wish we didn't have to stop.'

'Even I cannot drive for days without rest,' he said dryly. 'You need to relax and leave the worrying to me.'

'But you're not worrying.'

'A worry is merely a problem which hasn't been solved.' He undid her seat belt, and there was a sardonic gleam in his eyes. 'If I see a problem, I solve it.'

Her heart banged against her chest. 'What if you don't see the problem before it hits you?'

'Then the reaction must be all the quicker.'

Leaning her head back against the seat of the car, she closed her eyes. Despite the sleep she'd managed to snatch, she felt mentally and physically exhausted, the strain of the past few weeks building to a crescendo. 'I'm so tired.'

'Hopefully you will sleep better tonight.'

'Yes.' Alexa turned to look at him. 'Thank you. I know I said I didn't want a bodyguard, but I never would have managed this journey without you. I can see that now.' She sensed his immediate withdrawal.

'You are my responsibility.'

In other words he was just doing the job he was being paid to do, and he didn't want her to forget that. Unreasonably disappointed by his reaction, she climbed down from the vehicle and followed him into the tent.

'Well, I envy your stamina. I don't think I have the energy to eat. I'll just go straight to bed, and—' She broke off with a gasp of shock as she walked into the tent and saw the bed. 'Oh my goodness! It's like something out of an Arabian fantasy.'

'Indeed.' Karim opened a bottle of water and handed her a drink. 'The tourists like it. It is the honeymoon suite, I believe.'

Alexa stared at the huge bed draped in jewel-coloured silk and velvet cushions, and felt the colour heat her cheeks. Arabian antiques and elaborate rugs gave the tent a warm, intimate feel. It was clearly a place for lovers. 'Won't we be conspicuous staying here?'

'No one will be looking for you in the honeymoon suite. You're not married yet.'

The *yet* hung between them, and she gazed at him for a moment, noting the sudden tension in his broad shoulders.

It was ridiculous, she thought frantically, to be so sexually aware of a man when she was about to marry another. She had to stop thinking about Karim in that way. Just because he'd been kind, didn't mean that he was thinking…

'We should eat.' His voice sounded unnaturally harsh, and the fact that he turned away from her made her wonder if he'd somehow sensed the way she was feeling.

Was he shocked? Embarrassed? Probably, because she certainly was.

'I'm not really hungry.'

'Sit down, Alexa.' He sounded tired, and he rubbed the tips

of his bronzed fingers over his forehead as if to relieve the tension. 'You must eat. We have almost two days of travel ahead of us, and you ate virtually nothing today.'

'All right. Just something small.'

She wasn't aware that he'd communicated with anyone, and yet moments later several staff entered the tent, bearing a selection of dishes which they placed on the rug. Once they were alone again, Alexa knelt down. 'So this place is actually a hotel?'

'Zangrar is proving a surprisingly popular tourist destination.' Karim picked up a dish and transferred several delicacies to her plate. 'These desert encampments appeal to the romantic nature of tourists. They have a chance to swim, go dune driving, ride a camel and spend a night in the desert under the stars.'

'Tourism was the Sultan's idea?'

'He has driven much of the commercial development, yes. It is important to look forward to the time when our natural resources run out.'

'It's wonderful that he cares so much about the future of Zangrar.' Alexa stared at the food on her plate without touching it. 'My father was the same. He was passionate about Rovina—' She stopped suddenly, horrified with herself. Why was she talking about her father?

'His death must have been a great loss to the country.'

'I miss him every day.' Her hand shook, and Karim reached out and gently removed the plate that she was holding.

'Much of the security of childhood comes from parental love. You were deprived of that.' His astute observation surprised her.

'Yes, it was hard.'

'At least you had your uncle to care for you.'

Alexa felt herself hovering on the brink of unfamiliar territory. This was the point where she should tell him the truth. She *wanted* to tell him the truth. But trusting anyone was so alien that she just couldn't persuade her mouth to form the words. She just couldn't take that final plunge. So she stayed silent, and was just about to change the subject altogether when she heard the sound of a vehicle outside.

She turned her head swiftly towards the doorway of the tent. 'Did you hear something?'

'A car. Probably late arrivals.'

But her sense of danger was so finely tuned that she just *knew*, and she stood up so quickly that she tipped several of the dishes onto the floor. 'They've found us.'

Karim's eyes narrowed, but he rose to his feet. 'They will simply be tourists. Wait here. I will investigate.'

'No!' Forcing herself to think clearly, she grabbed his arm. 'Don't do that. Is there another exit? We need to get out of here before they find us.'

'Calm down.' Clearly believing that her reaction was wildly exaggerated, he gently removed his arm from her grip and strolled out of the tent.

Alexa didn't waste a moment in contemplation.

Her hands and knees shaking, she stuffed her hair under a hat and grabbed her knife. Hoping that the Sultan would agree to pay for the damage, she cut a hole in the back of the opulent tent and slipped out into the night.

She wasn't waiting to see who the visitors were. She already knew.

And she ran. As quickly as she could in unfamiliar terrain she ran, past a swimming pool, between the sloping palm-trees and out towards the desert. She didn't know where she was going, but she hoped she'd be able to find somewhere to hide. Her heart was pounding, her mouth was dry and she stumbled twice as she ran in the darkness.

There were shouts from beyond the tents and then an explosion of gunfire behind her, and Alexa froze. She'd left Karim to handle them alone.

She looked over her shoulder, torn by indecision. He hadn't believed her and that wasn't all his fault. She hadn't told him everything, had she? And now, because of her, he was in danger.

Cursing herself for not forcing him to leave with her, she turned back towards the tents, but then she heard the roar of a car engine and headlights came towards her.

Her heart pounded and a feeling of helpless despair swamped her.

They'd found her. And out here, trapped in unfamiliar terrain, she could do little to defend herself.

It was all over.

Unable to run, she stood staring at those headlights—*stood waiting to die.*

'Alexa! Move!' Karim's harsh tone penetrated her haze of fear, but she was shaking so much she couldn't do anything. He opened the door, jumped down from the vehicle and swung her bodily into his arms. 'Now is *not* the time to stand still.' Behaving as if she weighed nothing, he virtually threw her into the passenger seat, and was back behind the wheel and stamping hard on the accelerator before she'd even had time to catch her breath.

'Do your seat belt up,' he bit out sharply. 'In the dark I can't be sure I'll avoid the holes in the ground.'

Her hands shaking, she did as she instructed and then gasped as she saw the stain spreading on his sleeve. 'You're hurt.'

'It's just a scratch.'

'It's *all* my fault. I shouldn't have let you come with me—'

'Are they behind us?'

Alexa glanced over her shoulder and saw lights. 'Yes. They're following.'

'Then we go where they won't be able to follow.' His tone grim, Karim spun the wheel and took the vehicle off-road.

Realising his intention, she clutched at her seat and looked at him in disbelief. 'You're planning to go dune driving in the dark?'

'It will make it harder for them to follow. There is an old Bedouin camel-trail not far from here. If we can make it to there, then we will be safe.' He took the vehicle up the side of the dune in much the same way as he had done that morning, only this time there was no laughter, and she was horribly aware of the stain darkening the fabric of his shirt.

'I need to stop the bleeding. Does this car have a first-aid kit?'

'Under the seat. Leave it. They're still behind us.' As they reached the top of the dune, he glanced in the mirror and gave a faint smile of triumph. 'But not any more. They didn't tackle it at the right angle and they have rolled to the bottom. Let's move.'

'Your arm—'

'Hold on.' He took the vehicle down the other side, driving with more care than he had during daylight hours. 'Tell me who they are. *Who are those people?*'

'I don't know. Someone working for my uncle. It's always someone different. To be on the safe side, I just suspect everyone.'

Karim muttered something in his own language, and then switched back to English. 'Are you telling me that he employs different people to kill you?'

'I *did* tell you that my life was under threat, but you didn't believe me.'

'Reasons might have helped.'

'Never mind that now. Oh, God, there's blood everywhere.' She dug around under the seat, found the first-aid kit and flipped it open. 'You're going to have to stop so that I can look at your arm, Karim.'

He ignored her. 'Talk to me, Alexa! *Why* would your uncle want you dead?'

'It's complicated, and you need to concentrate on driving.'

Rummaging through the first-aid kit, she pulled out a bandage. 'Is the bullet in the wound?'

'No. I've already told you, it's just a scratch. *Answer my question*. What are we dealing with here?'

'Cain and Abel,' she muttered, and he glanced at her sharply. 'Jealousy between brothers? That is what this is about?'

Alexa ripped the packaging from the bandage. 'His brother— my father—is dead. I'm the last remaining obstacle between him and the throne of Rovina.'

'He already rules Rovina.'

'As Regent. He wants to rule in his own right. He's always wanted that. If I reach my twenty-fifth birthday, then I take over as ruler. He isn't going to let that happen.' She steadied herself as the vehicle plunged and bounced on the uneven ground. 'You need to stop so that I can see what I'm doing.'

'We're not stopping until I decide that it's safe.'

'Then I'll just have to bandage it over your clothes. I'm sorry you were hurt because of me.'

He glanced towards her, his eyes gleaming dark and dangerous in the dim light of the car. 'I'm sorry I didn't believe you when you said that you were in danger. When it is safe, we will stop and you will start talking. And this time I'll be listening hard.'

Her hands shook as she bandaged his arm. 'We won't be safe until we reach the Citadel.'

'We will. The desert is a very unforgiving place for those without knowledge. This is an old Bedouin route. If we drive along here, we will reach the caves and we can rest there.' Karim reached out a hand, punched a number into a satellite phone and then proceeded to speak rapidly in a language that she didn't understand. When he finally broke the connection, she looked at him expectantly.

'What was that about?'

'I have asked for a security team to pick up those men and

question them.' His expression was grim as he gripped the wheel with his hand and drove hard and fast through the desert. 'There may be others.'

The caves formed a dark, forbidding labyrinth at the base of the huge sandstone-cliffs. Alexa leaned forward, peering through the darkness. 'We're going in there?'

'Yes.' Karim parked the vehicle out of sight of the road and winced as he reached for a torch and some blankets. 'No one will look for us here.'

Alexa felt her stomach lurch at the thought of all that dark, confined space, but said nothing. She knew that they needed to get out of sight, and she was worried about Karim's arm. 'Let's go, then.'

She followed him into the entrance of the caves. 'Shall we just stop here?' Her voice echoed and he flashed the torch towards the back of the cave where the rocks narrowed.

'Through there is a smaller chamber. We'll spend the night there. It will be warmer.'

And darker and more closed in. Alexa stood for a moment, finding it impossible to make her feet move. Then she remembered that they were in this situation because of her, and forced herself to follow him through the narrow gap, reminding herself that she wasn't locked in.

There was a way out.

Karim checked that the ground was dry and then dropped the blankets. 'Sit down.'

'*You* sit down. I need to look at your arm.' She undid the emergency dressing she'd applied and waited while he pulled off his shirt. Blood oozed from the wound, and she cursed softly and pressed down hard, staunching the flow. 'It's bleeding a lot. I'll clean it and dress it, but I suspect that it could have done with some stitches.'

'So blood is yet another thing that doesn't frighten you?'

'Don't be ridiculous. Can you shine the torch on this so that I can see what I'm doing?' Removing what she needed from the first-aid kit, Alexa swabbed the wound and took a closer look. 'You're right. The bullet just grazed the skin. I'll clean it, but you probably need some antibiotics.'

'And how can a princess, who supposedly isn't interested in anything more than fast cars and high heels, be so adept at first aid?' He watched as she carefully applied a sterile dressing to his arm and bound it firmly.

'I've spent a lot of time working at the local hospital. William hasn't invested any money in healthcare since he became Regent. The hospitals are struggling—no money, no staff. Morale is rock bottom. I help out when I can.'

'You work in the hospital?'

'As a volunteer.' Alexa closed the first-aid kit. 'I'm not trained, or anything. I would have loved to have been a doctor, but there was never any chance of that.'

He studied her for a moment, his expression forbidding. 'Sit down, Alexandra. It's time we talked about your uncle.'

Alexa sat down on the rug and tried not to think about the darkness. *They weren't closed in,* she reminded herself. 'I'm really sorry I got you into all this. I knew it was a mistake to take you with me.'

'I didn't give you a choice in the matter.' He sat down next to her. 'But clearly, I should have listened to you more carefully. I'm listening now, Alexa. Start talking.' The silence of the cave closed around them like a protective cocoon.

'I wouldn't know where to start.'

'Start with why you're marrying the Sultan.' He shone the torch towards her so that he could see her face. 'It doesn't have anything to do with the money or the status, does it?'

'I'm marrying the Sultan because it's my best chance of staying alive. You keep telling me that he's going to lock me behind the walls of the Citadel, and that's what I'm hoping for,' Alexa said softly. 'I want to reach my twenty-fifth birthday. I want to rule Rovina. Since my uncle took over, I've watched the country slowly crumble. He has diverted money away from the things that matter, like healthcare and education, and instead spends it on things that benefit only him. Like refurbishing the palace, and adding another priceless stallion to his stud farm. My uncle has stripped Rovina bare over the sixteen years since my father died.'

'So you're marrying the Sultan to escape?'

'In the short term, yes. In the longer term…' She hesitated and then gave a shrug. 'The Sultan is a powerful man, and I know he's turned Zangrar around in the past few years. If anyone can help me solve Rovina's problems, then it's him. His father and my father were friends. I just hope that's enough to persuade him to help.'

'Your uncle intends to prevent you from becoming Queen? This is the reason you believe he has tried to have you killed?'

It felt completely alien to confide in someone, and she sat for a moment, trying to find the words.

'I know it, Karim.' It was easier to talk in the semi-darkness. 'It started off as a campaign to discredit me with the public. He thought that if he made me look bad enough then no one would want me as ruler. My wild image was orchestrated by him. Starting with those awful photographs of me topless.'

'The photographs were fake?'

'No.' Alexa curled her legs under her. 'They were real. It was the first and last time in my life that I allowed myself to trust another person. Let's just say that he was an actor, and he was good at his job. I was so lonely, and to have someone pay me attention…' She gave a short laugh. 'Not that that is an excuse for being stupid and gullible, I know.'

'You were manipulated?'

'My uncle paid him to be caught in a compromising situation

with me. They both did very well out of it. The actor's career took off, and the photographs were published again and again all over the world as an example of how I'd gone off the rails. Anyway, although the public was shocked, they still supported me. Perhaps they were tolerant because I'd lost my whole family. I don't know. Maybe they didn't like William. By then they could see that he had no commitment towards Rovina as a country. He just used his position to enhance his own lifestyle. Either way, he obviously decided he had to work a little harder. And that was when I suddenly became so accident prone.'

'Your car accidents—'

'On both occasions, someone tampered with the brakes.'

The breath hissed through his teeth. 'You are *sure?*'

'Yes. I was just angry that I let it happen twice. After that, I stopped driving, or I borrowed cars at short notice.'

'You didn't try to escape? Drive over the border?'

'I was watched all the time. I was lucky if I managed to get beyond the palace walls. When I was little he locked me in.'

Karim muttered something under his breath. 'And that is why you hate locked doors?'

'Yes. Silly, really. It's just a psychological thing. I like to know that I can get out if I want to. He only did it when I was little. As I grew older I was a little harder to contain. He wanted me dead, but if he couldn't have that then he wanted me where he could see me. It became a game of cat and mouse. I'd disguise myself and find different ways of slipping out.'

'He always caught you?'

'He has supporters. Greedy people, like him, who are interested in themselves and not Rovina.'

'The speedboat accident?'

'*Not* an accident.'

With a driven sigh, Karim ran a hand over the back of his neck. 'The time you were removed unconscious from a nightclub?'

'I was drugged. I wasn't even in the nightclub at the time. They staged the photographs, but by then most people just assumed I'd gone off the rails because of my parents' death. "The rebel princess" they called me.' She laughed. 'I sort of grew into the role. I had to, in order to stay alive.'

'You had no one to protect you?'

'You have to remember that most people just thought what you thought—that I was a bit of a wild child. No one really understood what my uncle was capable of.' Alexa felt a lump in her throat. 'Every time I allowed myself to trust someone, it proved to be a mistake, so I stopped trusting. It was safer for everyone if I just lived my life alone.'

'*Why* did you not tell me any of this before now?' He sounded angry and she couldn't blame him for that.

He'd just been shot because of her.

'I did try telling you my uncle was following us.'

'But you didn't give me details, did you?' Karim stretched out a hand and lifted her chin so that she was forced to look at him. 'You omitted all the facts that would have given your story credibility.'

'I *wanted* to tell you,' Alexa murmured, 'and several times I almost did. But you have to understand that in my situation *not* talking is the only thing that keeps you alive. For the past sixteen years, I haven't been able to trust anyone. I disciplined myself to stay silent, and I can't suddenly change that.'

Karim let his hand drop, clearly struggling to absorb the enormity of what she was telling him. 'If William is willing to go to those lengths to keep the throne for himself, then there must have been times when you've wondered whether he could have played a part in your father's death.'

She stared into the semi-darkness. 'He had my parents killed.' Somehow the eerie silence of the cave made her statement all the more dramatic.

Then she heard him draw breath. 'I can see how it would be easy for you to believe that, given the way he has treated you, but—'

'I was there.' She turned her head to look at him and in the dim torchlight his arrogant profile looked hard and forbidding. 'I saw it happen.'

'You *witnessed* the explosion that killed your parents?'

'It was meant to kill me, too. We'd been staying at our country house for the weekend. Just as we were about to leave I remembered that I'd forgotten my doll.' Her heart-rate trebled, and suddenly her palms felt sweaty and her mouth was dry. This wasn't something she talked about. She *never* talked about it. 'I went back to the house and the car exploded.'

Another long silence followed her shaky declaration, and suddenly Alexa found herself just longing for him to comfort her, as he had during her nightmare, but he sat still as if her words had somehow rendered him immobile.

Finally he spoke. 'You are sure your uncle was involved?'

'Well, I had no way of proving it, of course—but, yes, I'm sure. I saw him immediately after the explosion.' She gave a shiver. 'I'll never forget the look on his face, Karim. He wasn't sad or even shocked. The only time he looked shocked was when they found me and brought me to him. And even though I was so young I just *knew* that he'd intended for me to die, too.'

'You were eight years old.'

'He wanted my whole family dead. He hated my father. Hated him for everything he had. And I was terrified,' Alexa confessed. 'To begin with I tried to talk to people, but they just thought I was hysterical. I'd witnessed my parents' death, after all. Then someone I confided in just disappeared. Although I was young, I realized that talking to anyone was dangerous.'

'I can't believe he intended to harm you. You were a child.'

'But a dangerous child.' Alexa's chin lifted. 'My father's child. Rovina is in my blood, and my uncle knew it.'

'You were impossibly young to find yourself so alone.' Karim shook his head in disbelief. 'I'm surprised it didn't break you.'

Alexa was silent for a moment, remembering how terrified and lonely she'd been. 'There were days when I was desperate for someone to just hold me and tell me that everything was going to be all right.'

There was a long silence, and the light flickered as Karim put the torch down on the rug. Then he reached out and lifted her, pulling her onto his lap and curving his arms around her. '*I* am holding you, *habibati,*' he breathed softly, stroking her hair away from her face and guiding her head onto his shoulder with his hand. 'And everything *is* going to be all right, I promise you that. Your uncle will not come near you again. You have my word on it.'

'I—what if the Sultan doesn't believe me?'

Karim was silent for a moment. 'He *will* believe you, I can assure you of that.'

He seemed so convinced that Alexa felt herself slowly relax, and it felt so good to be held that for a moment she just lay there, enjoying the rare indulgence of letting someone else take control. 'It feels funny talking about it. I keep waiting for you to stand up and confess that you're not who you say you are. That you're actually working for my uncle.'

His arms tightened. 'I can understand that you have been extremely traumatized by your experience, but I promise you that you *can* trust me.'

Alexa closed her eyes and snuggled closer and his warm, masculine scent made her stomach quiver. 'Have you any idea how it feels to have someone on your side after a lifetime of being alone?' For the first time in as long as she could remember, she felt safe. 'How is your arm?'

'Barely hurting.'

She smiled in the darkness. 'You're lying.'

'Tell me about your dream, Alexa.'

Her smile faded. 'I don't want to talk about that.'

'Try.' He smoothed a hand gently over her hair, and shifted slightly so that he held her even closer. 'For me, *habibati*.'

'After they were killed, I suppose I was in shock. I just wanted to wind the clock back. I wished I'd made my parents go back for the doll while I stayed in the car. I wished something had happened to stop us leaving at that exact moment.' Alexa paused, hollowed out by sadness. 'That's the dream I have. Time and time again I race towards the car to warn them, but I'm too late. I'm always too late.'

'I cannot *believe* I didn't discover any of this when I was in Rovina.'

'You weren't looking.'

'Why was no one able to protect you?'

'My uncle is very, very clever and he had many supporters. And, don't forget, he didn't exactly present me in a good light. By the time he'd finished, most people were wondering how a princess who couldn't even drive her car straight could possibly run a country. I knew I had to get away if I was ever going to survive. I pinned all my hopes on this marriage to the Sultan. It was my only escape route.'

'And you're taking it.'

'Do you blame me?' She lifted her head and saw Karim's eyes glitter in the torchlight.

'No,' he said harshly. 'After everything you've told me, I do not blame you.'

'You saved my life tonight.' Unable to help herself, she reached out a hand and touched his face, feeling the roughness of his jaw beneath her fingers. 'I just panicked and ran.'

'You have no reason to thank me.' Suddenly he seemed tense. 'It is my job to protect you. And I *will* protect you, Alexa. You can be sure of that.'

His job. Alexa felt despair and disappointment mingle, and let her hand drop. What had she expected? Comfort wasn't part of his job description. 'I don't know what the Sultan told you when he gave you this mission, but I don't suppose the brief included getting yourself shot. It was hard for me to trust you, but I'm glad I did. You're the first person I've met who hasn't betrayed that trust. Thank you.'

'You are safe, and that is what matters.'

She knew she ought to move. He'd taken her in his arms to give her comfort, nothing more. But she couldn't bring herself to move away from his warmth and strength. *In a minute,* she promised herself, her eyes sliding nervously around the shadows of the cave. 'Do you think they'll find us?'

'No. You should get some sleep.'

'I don't want to sleep.'

'Because of the nightmares? I suspect you only have the dream when you are wound up and tense.'

Sensing that he was about to tip her off his lap, she reached up and wound her arms round his neck. 'Can we stay like this? Just for a minute?'

His muscles were rock hard and rigid beneath her quivering body. 'Alexa—'

'Please, Karim?' She whispered the words against the smooth, warm skin of his neck and felt his throat move.

'Alexa, we can't—'

'I just want you to hug me, that's all. Do you know how long it is since anyone hugged me? I was eight years old, and I barely remember it.'

He didn't answer for a moment, and then shifted his body and lay down, taking her with him. 'I will hold you and you will sleep.'

He made it sound like an order, and she gave a contented smile because only Karim would think of ordering a person to sleep.

But at least he was still holding her.

'Do you always try and control everything that goes on around you?'

'Always.'

She felt his muscles flex as he reached for a blanket and covered them both. 'Sleep, Alexa.'

The darkness suddenly seemed intimate and welcoming, and she wondered why she'd ever been afraid of the caves.

But the moment his arms came round her, and she felt his hard, athletic body brushing intimately against hers, she knew that there was no hope of sleep.

Why did she feel like this?

It was just because she'd confided in him, she told herself, because he'd saved her and listened and offered sympathy. These feelings inside her were there simply because, for the first time in her lonely life, she'd dared to share her problems with another person.

It was just gratitude.

But the slow, dangerous curl of warmth low in her pelvis didn't feel anything like gratitude, and she shifted slightly to ease the electric buzz in her body.

'Stop moving.' Karim sounded equally tense, and she was just about to pull away from him when he gave a low groan, rolled her on her back and brought his mouth down hard on hers, his kiss hungry and urgent. His hand slid into her hair and cupped the back of her head, holding her firmly while his mouth seduced hers with shocking expertise, demanding a response from her.

And she gave freely. It didn't enter her head to push him away, because why would she want to stop something that felt so completely right?

He kissed in exactly the way she remembered, and her response was as wild and uncontrolled as it had been before. Excitement exploded through her, and she dug her fingers into his hard, strong shoulders, holding on as he drove her wild. She felt helpless and out of control, and when she felt his hand slide over her taut nipple she cried out against his mouth and arched in urgent invitation.

He knew exactly where to touch her—how to touch her—to derive the maximum response from her, and Alexa shifted against the blanket in an attempt to relieve the maddening ache between her legs. And he must have known what he was doing to her, because his hand moved lower still, and she felt the gentle brush of his fingers touching her intimately. And that almost agonizing intimacy jerked her out of her stupor.

She couldn't do this, could she?

No matter how right it felt, it was still wrong.

Karim couldn't be part of her future.

'No.' Never had it felt so hard to say that word, and her fingers closed over the hard muscle of his arm as if she knew that she was never going to have the will-power to do this by words alone. 'No. We have to stop. We have to stop now.' Before she was unable to stop. And she was already so close to that point.

He broke the kiss briefly, but only to look deep into her eyes, and the intensity of that look and the warmth of his breath was as seductive as the touch of his mouth. 'You want to stop?'

No. No, she didn't. *But she had to.* 'I don't want this.'

'That's a lie.' Dismissing her rejection with his usual confidence, his mouth claimed hers again and she felt herself descending into a thick, sensual fog that threatened to consume her.

'No, Karim.' Denying her own sensuality, she dragged her mouth away from his and this time she turned her head. 'You have to stop! It's not right. I'm marrying the Sultan. We shouldn't be doing this.'

'You want me.' His arrogant statement left no room for denial, and she didn't even bother trying.

'Yes. But that doesn't change anything.' Faced with the most impossible decision, she shifted away from him slightly, wishing that she knew how to calm the reaction of her body. 'I— This should never have happened. I can't be with you, Karim. I'm not the sort of woman who can sleep with one man and then marry another. It wouldn't be right.'

She was still a virgin and that, at least, she could give to the Sultan.

He was silent for a moment, his powerful body tense over hers, his breathing harsh and laboured as he struggled to exercise control. Then he rolled away from her and she caught a glimpse of his face. The expression in his eyes was fierce and his jaw was tense. And then he flicked off the torch and they were plunged into darkness.

Now what?

Alexa started miserably into the inky blackness, not knowing what to do or say. She wanted to reach out and touch him, but knew that she had no right to do that, but it was suddenly vitally important that he knew just how much he meant to her.

'You're the first person in sixteen years I've been able to trust,' she said softly, the darkness giving her the courage to say things she never would have been able to say in daylight. 'I didn't dare trust anyone else or let them close, because they always had a reason for being with me and that reason was always something to my disadvantage. It's been so different with you. You insisted on protecting me even though I didn't want your protection. Even though we've only spent a short time together, I feel I really know you. You're the first friend I've ever had. And, if things were different, you would have been my first lover.'

'Enough, Alexa.' His voice was raw, or perhaps the darkness simply exaggerated the emotions. 'Get some rest now.'

The disappointment lay inside her like a heavy weight that couldn't be shifted.

She sat still for a moment, trying to reason with herself. What had she expected—a declaration of love? No, not that. But *something* that indicated that her feelings hadn't been entirely one sided, because she knew that they hadn't been. *He cared for her; she knew he did.* And yet he hadn't once expressed those feelings.

But was that so surprising?

She was about to become the Sultan's wife.

Perhaps he believed that the only way he was going to be able to watch her marry another man was if he denied those feelings.

But she wished, even if it was just for this one night, that he'd told her how he felt. It would have made everything easier, somehow, even though it wouldn't have changed a thing.

She was on her way to marry the Sultan.

But for the first time ever, that marriage felt less like a sanctuary and more like a sacrifice.

Battling with unfulfilled sexual desire, and a *serious* attack of conscience for the first time in his life, Karim lay still until the sound of her breathing indicated that she had fallen asleep.

Her words troubled him more than he would have thought possible.

What was it she had said—that he was the first person that hadn't betrayed her trust?

And yet that wasn't true, was it?

His role as her bodyguard had been secondary to the main purpose of his mission: *to persuade her not to marry the Sultan.*

But now that he had the facts he could see that Alexa's character had been grossly misrepresented. And, knowing the truth about her, he had no doubt that she would make the Sultan a perfectly good wife. She was clearly loyal, resourceful and resilient. And she was remarkably well-adjusted, considering the considerable hardship she'd suffered since the death of her family.

Ironically enough, perhaps the only blot on her copybook was her reaction to *him*. She was about to marry another man, and yet she'd been openly and unashamedly passionate.

But she *had* stopped, he reminded himself, shifting with frustration as he recalled just how much restraint that action had demanded of him. And the fact that she'd stopped had to be a point in her favour.

Knowing how passionate she was, he didn't for a moment believe that she was a virgin, but at least she'd had the decency not to indulge in a little hot desert sex with him, despite the powerful chemistry.

Karim thought for a moment, his eyes sliding to her sleeping form.

What reason was there for him to feel guilty? He had merely done what needed to be done. No blame attached to him for the fact that she'd been so grossly misrepresented by her uncle. It was clear that his mission was no longer necessary, and equally clear what should happen next.

There was really no reason for the Sultan not to marry her.

CHAPTER EIGHT

ALEXA woke to find light seeping into the cave.

She sat up, feeling tired and gritty eyed, having spent most of the night trying not to reach out and touch Karim. Part of her wished she hadn't stopped him. It would have been the first time in her life that she'd actually done something that *she* wanted.

But she couldn't be that selfish.

Her responsibility was to the Sultan and the people of Rovina. Now that a new life was in sight, she couldn't help but dream that a man as powerful as the Sultan might be able to help her transform her beloved homeland.

Shafts of daylight penetrated the cave, and now she could see where they had spent the night. And there was no sign of Karim.

Wondering where he was, she was about to call his name when she heard the unmistakable sound of a helicopter landing outside the cave.

Alexa was on her feet in an instant, her legs shaking and her mouth dry with fear.

They'd found her.

While she'd been lying in Karim's arms, feeling safe and protected for the first time in her life, they'd been tracking her.

And now she and Karim were trapped in the cave.

Shaking with panic, and cursing herself for her stupidity, she sprinted towards the entrance, but strong arms caught her and prevented her from running outside.

'It's all right. There is nothing to frighten you.' Karim's voice was rough. 'I called the helicopter. In the circumstances, I thought it best if we get you away from here as fast as possible before your uncle discovers that he has failed and tries again.'

It took a moment for his words to sink in, and then the breath left her in a sigh of relief. '*You* called the helicopter?'

'That's right.'

'So—I'm leaving? Are you coming, too?'

He hesitated, and for a moment his fingers tightened on her arms. Then he released her and took a step backwards. 'No. They will fly you directly to the Citadel. You will be safe there.'

'I don't want to go without you.' Alexa spoke without thinking and then turned away, embarrassed at having revealed so much. For so long she'd been used to hiding her feelings. She'd trusted no one—*relied on no one but herself.* But all that had changed during her two days in the desert with Karim.

Everything had changed last night.

For the first time in her life since her parents had been killed, someone had been there for her, protecting her and watching over her. For the first time in her life she'd really talked to someone, and someone had held her when she'd had the dream.

And now she had to say goodbye.

So why couldn't she move?

This was the moment she'd been dreaming of for so long. So why was it so impossibly hard to step into the helicopter?

Gratitude?

Alexa glanced at Karim's strong, handsome face. *No, it wasn't gratitude.*

Now that they were due to part, she knew that it was something so much more than that.

She knew that it was love.

The realization shocked her, and she made a little sound, confused and horrified. This was *not* what she wanted.

'Alexa—' He seemed tense, too, and when one of the soldiers approached them he lifted a hand in a silent command that made them stop in their tracks. 'It will be all right.'

How could it possibly be all right?

And then she realized that he was talking about her safety.

He didn't know that she was in love with him. Or maybe he did, and he was embarrassed. He guarded the Sultan, didn't he? Knowing that the Sultan's wife had feelings for him wasn't going to make his job easy.

She *had* to pull herself together. But she'd been deprived of these feelings for so long that it was almost impossible to give them up.

'Yes.' Allowing herself the luxury of one last look, her eyes lingered on the dark stubble that shadowed his hard jaw, and then lifted to his mouth—that same mouth that had kissed her senseless in the night. Would she be able to forget? *When the Sultan kissed her, would she think of Karim?*

Afraid that if she stood there a moment longer she'd make an even bigger fool of herself, Alexa turned and walked quickly towards the waiting helicopter, trying to ignore the pull that made her want to turn her head one more time.

Don't look back, she told herself. *Don't look back. You're not going to be that weak.*

She would marry the Sultan as she'd planned. She'd do it for Rovina and for her beloved father's memory, and she would hide her feelings for Karim because that was what had to be done.

What choice did she have?

Hands urged her aboard the helicopter and Alexa responded

passively, numbed by the strange feeling of loss that consumed her.

She was strapped into her seat, given ear protectors, and then the helicopter rose above the sand.

And the pull became impossible to resist.

All her resolutions exploded to nothing, and she turned her head to look, and through the mist of sand she saw him standing there, his legs planted firmly apart in a typically arrogant stance as he watched her departure.

He'd protected her, given her hope, taught her that love was possible, even for her.

She should be feeling happy and grateful.

So why did she feel as though she'd lost everything a second time?

Had Alexa not been so distracted by thoughts of Karim, she would have been excited by her first view of the Citadel of Zangrar. From the air it spread beneath them in majestic splendour, the walls of buff-coloured stone high and imposing. And inside the walls of the Citadel was the Sultan's palace with its high domes and graceful lines.

Her stomach churned, and suddenly she remembered all the things that Karim had told her about the Sultan.

He gave an order and it was done.

No one would dare argue with him.

The Sultan's expectations of her role would not extend beyond the bedroom.

As those words filled her head, Alexa was suddenly swamped with a feeling of cold dread.

It was all very well talking of duty and responsibility, but with reality this close she was suddenly terrified. What if the Sultan refused to help her?

What if she'd simply swapped one set of problems for another?

What if her new life was worse than the old?

And then she thought of what her uncle had done to her and to Rovina, and realized that nothing could be worse.

All the same, she was so subdued that she barely noticed that they'd landed until eight armed-guards surrounded her and then escorted her swiftly to the Sultan's private quarters within the palace.

Jittery with nerves, she glanced around her, waiting anxiously for the moment when the Sultan would appear. 'Will I meet His Excellency soon?'

'Not before the wedding, Your Highness.' An army of women had been assigned to look after her, and they bustled around her now, clucking over the dusty clothes that she'd worn in the desert and adding rose petals to steaming bath-water.

'I can take a bath by myself.' She wasn't used to being waited on, but no one took any notice of her wishes and soon she was lying in the luxuriously scented water, the warmth and fragrance driving the memories of the sand and the heat from her mind. But no amount of washing or massage removed the memory of Karim. It was as if he'd somehow left a mark of ownership on her. When she closed her eyes, she immediately felt his hands on her skin and his mouth on hers.

The memory triggered a stab of panic, and she sat up in the bath. She couldn't do it.

It wasn't the wedding, it was—the rest of it.

What had Karim said? *The Sultan had an extremely high sex-drive.*

Somehow, when he'd first said it, the words hadn't really registered in her brain. They just hadn't meant anything.

But now, after what she'd shared with Karim…

What if, when the time came, she just couldn't let another man touch her in that way?

Perhaps, if she could just meet him, she thought miserably,

and discover what sort of man he was. Would that make the whole situation less awful—or more awful?

Her brain magnifying the horrors of her position with each passing second, Alexa turned on impulse to the women who were preparing various massage oils. 'I'd like to talk to the Sultan.'

The women gasped with shock, as if she'd made an outrageous request.

'Unfortunately that will not be possible, Your Highness,' one of them muttered. 'It is bad luck for the Sultan to lay eyes on his bride before the wedding.'

Even more bad luck to lay eyes on her after it, Alexa thought gloomily, staring at the rose petals that floated on the surface of the water. What if he took one look at her and ran?

If it hadn't been for the duty she owed her country, she would have run herself.

'The wedding will take place tomorrow, Your Highness. After that you will have the Sultan's full attention.' The women exchanged knowing looks, and Alexa sighed with frustration.

So she wasn't even going to be given the chance to meet the Sultan before she married him.

Sinking back under the scented bath-water, she stared at the rose petals floating in the water and wondered whether there had ever been a more miserable bride.

This should have been a moment of triumph and relief.

She'd reached the Citadel safely. Nothing could stand between her and marriage to the Sultan.

But somewhere on the journey she'd given away her heart, and there seemed no hope of getting it back. Now she knew how love felt, marrying another man felt completely wrong.

The bath was followed by a long, luxurious massage with aromatic oils, and eventually Alexa was tucked up in a large, comfortable bed in a room with the floor area of a small house. It was so different from the starkness and fear that had surrounded her life in Rovina that, had she not met Karim, she would have felt extremely relaxed and content with her situation.

But she *had* met Karim.

She'd fallen in love with him.

And that had changed the way she felt about everything.

She woke early.

The hot desert sun poured through the arched windows, illuminating the richness of the fabrics that draped the bed, and Alexa just lay for a moment, thinking.

Where was he and what was he doing right now?

Filled with an almost agonizing longing to see Karim, she turned her head and stared towards the window.

Was he somewhere close?

Was he back guarding the Sultan?

Was he thinking of her?

Alexa sat up in bed, realizing that it was her birthday.

Her twenty-fourth birthday.

And today she was going to marry the Sultan.

As if to remind her of that fact, there was a soft tap on the door and the room was suddenly filled with people eager to help her prepare for the wedding.

After that there was no more opportunity for quiet reflection, and the next few hours flashed by as women attended to her hair and make-up and made final adjustments to the fitting of her wedding dress.

Alexa stared down at herself, looking at the simplicity of the silk dress. What was it Karim had said—that a woman came to her husband in a simple dress, denoting honesty?

At the beginning of the journey she'd had no problem with that. She'd had every intention of being honest with him.

But now? How truthful was it to marry a man while loving another?

The nerves in her stomach stirred, and she hoped desperately that Karim would not be present at the wedding. What if he was? And what if she couldn't hide her feelings for him? Hadn't Karim told her that the Sultan was fiercely possessive? Just what would such a man do if he discovered that she was in love with someone else?

'Your Highness is very pale.' The girl in charge of her make-up snapped her fingers, and a woman stepped forward with a selection of jars and pots. She selected one and rubbed the colour vigorously into Alexa's ashen cheeks. 'You should not be nervous. You are incredibly beautiful. The Sultan will be pleased.'

The Sultan will be pleased.

That information didn't cheer Alexa in the least. In fact, she felt sicker than ever. Now that the moment of her marriage was approaching, she was beginning to wonder whether she'd be able to go through with it.

She'd waited for this moment for so long, and yet now it had finally arrived everything had changed. And she knew who was responsible for that change.

Karim.

Her feelings for him had exploded out of nowhere, but they were so powerful that the thought of being with another man seemed unnatural.

But a life with Karim wasn't an option, was it?

Her father had wanted her to marry the Sultan, and it was the right thing to do.

Alexa stood, silent and unresisting, as the team of women finished adjusting her make-up to their satisfaction, and then covered her head and shoulders with several sheer veils.

'The Sultan cannot look upon his bride until the vows have been exchanged,' one of them explained, and then she curtsied low. 'You are ready for His Excellency. If Your Highness would follow me.'

The floor had been liberally sprinkled with scented rose petals, and Alexa forced herself to put one foot in front of the other, her shoes moving silently over the flowery carpet.

She was led into a brightly lit courtyard, and realized with a start of surprise that the wedding was going to be held outside. A small group of people had gathered, waiting, and her eyes searched nervously for the Sultan.

One man stood out from the others. He wore robes and a traditional head covering and had his back to her, but she knew, even without an introduction, that he was the Sultan. It wasn't just the way that those around were deferring to him that revealed his identity, but the way he held himself, with authority and command.

Breathless with nerves, Alexa waited for him to turn and face her, but he stood still, and the women urged her forward.

'The Sultan cannot look upon his bride until the ceremony has taken place,' one of them muttered, guessing at the reason for her hesitancy.

Alexa's despair grew.

So not only was she going to marry a man she hadn't met, she wasn't even going to see him before the wedding.

At least there was no sign of Karim, so that was something to be grateful for. She wasn't going to have to make her vows with the man she loved looking on. She'd been spared that agony.

The ceremony began, and because Alexa didn't understand a word of what was being said they prompted her and she gave the responses that were required of her, in English, barely registering the deep, masculine tones of the man standing by her side. Once, she stole a glance at him, but his profile was hidden from view.

And then everyone in the courtyard fell to their knees and bowed, and she realized that the ceremony had ended.

She was married to the Sultan.

It was done.

Everyone discreetly retreated into the palace, and she was left standing in the sunny courtyard with the tall, broad-shouldered man who was now her husband.

Was he ever going to look at her?

Or was he so angry at being forced into this marriage that they were going to live their lives as enemies?

Unable to bear the tension a moment longer, she closed her eyes in an attempt to calm herself down. And then she heard him move towards her and felt his hands lifting her veils, one by one, exposing her face to his gaze.

Alexa kept her eyes closed, hardly able to breathe.

His father and her father had forced this marriage on him, hadn't they? And, because of her situation, she'd done nothing to prevent it.

This situation was all her fault.

'I presume you are not intending to go through the whole of our marriage with your eyes closed, Alexa?' Now that he spoke in English, his low, masculine drawl was shockingly familiar, and her eyes flew wide-open as she stared in disbelief at the man in front of her.

'Karim?' For a moment she could do nothing more than whisper his name. Happiness bloomed inside her, and then withered instantly as her brain acknowledged the truth of the situation. Despite the intense heat and blazing sun, she suddenly felt deathly cold. 'Oh, God—it was you—'

'That's right.' He made no excuses. There were no denials— no apology—and she shook her head, still trying to digest the enormity of the truth.

He wasn't…

She'd thought…

She'd *trusted* him.

'But you—I—I told you *so* much.' More than she'd ever told another human being. She'd opened her soul to this man, not realizing who he was. 'I was honest with you.'

'And that is a good thing, not a matter for either regret or apology.'

'It is to me! What you did wasn't *right*, Karim.' The cold, numb feeling was fading, and in its place was hurt, vulnerability and the beginnings of anger. 'You deceived me! I trusted you, and you deceived me! You pretended to be someone else.'

'The deception was necessary.' He stood in front of her, arrogant and unrepentant, showing not a flicker of the softness he'd occasionally displayed during the journey. 'Being the Sultan's wife is a position of great responsibility. Did you really think I would have given that honour to a woman with the reputation that you possessed?'

His words sank slowly into her stunned brain. 'You never intended me to marry you, did you? That was why you chose to escort me personally. You were trying to make me change my mind.' She stared at him, her breathing shallow as everything fell into place with horrible clarity. 'All those stories you told me about the Sultan…' Her mouth was so dry she was forced to lick her lips in order to speak. 'All those desert experiences—they were just to put me off. You wanted me to back out, didn't you? And, just to be sure that no one else messed it up, you'd do the job yourself, was that right?' *He hadn't had feelings for her.* It had all been a sham.

With a casual lift of his broad shoulders, Karim dismissed the question as irrelevant. 'I am satisfied that most of your reputation was fabricated by your uncle.'

Most? In the back of her mind she registered the word, but she was too busy deciphering the bigger picture to pay attention to detail. 'It wasn't supposed to be a test, Karim.'

'It is behind us.'

'*It isn't behind us!*' There were goosebumps on her arms, and she gave a shiver. 'I can't believe I could have been so foolish. Why didn't I notice anything before? That man in the desert camp that first night—the one who bowed—he didn't recognize *me,* did he? He recognized you. And when we were in the cave and you called for that helicopter—' She broke off and shook her head with disbelief. 'We arrived at the Citadel in a matter of hours. This whole thing about having to journey across the desert…'

Two dark streaks illuminated his incredible bone structure, and for the first time since the conversation had started he actually looked mildly discomforted. 'I admit that communications in Zangrar are not quite as backward as I perhaps led you to believe. But it was necessary for me to spend time with you.'

'To frighten me off marrying the Sultan.'

He inhaled sharply. 'I did *not* frighten you.'

'But you tried, Karim.' Her voice shook with outrage and pain. 'You tried really, really hard. All that talk about snakes and the dangers of the desert. The pictures you painted of the Sultan—yourself—'

'None of that was fabricated. I merely exposed you to the truth of the situation.'

'Except that you omitted to introduce yourself fully.' She couldn't believe she'd actually been so gullible, and suddenly she needed to know everything. 'Tell me the truth. How long would it have taken us to reach the Citadel from the airport?'

'Not long.'

'How long?'

'A short helicopter transfer.'

As the deeper implication of his words sank into her numb brain she shook her head in disbelief. 'There was no need for us to be in the desert. We exposed ourselves to unnecessary risk. *You* exposed me to risk!'

'At the time I was not aware that you were in danger. And I would have protected you. I *did* protect you.'

'That does not excuse what you did, Karim! You let me lean on you. I trusted you and you betrayed me.'

'How? When?' His handsome face was all hard lines and unyielding strength. 'You reached out to me, Alexa. That night in the tent when you had the nightmare, you asked for comfort and I gave it. When you were attacked, you asked for my protection and I gave it. In what way did I betray your trust?'

'By not being honest about who you were.' She felt shattered, vulnerable and horribly exposed.

'If you had known my identity you would doubtless not have been so open, and we would therefore not now be married.'

'Yes, we would. There was never an option for you to stop the marriage.'

He gave a grim smile. 'Believe me, Alexa, I could have stopped it.'

Still bruised, she backed away from him. 'So why didn't you?' She sounded like a sulky child, and he studied her for a moment, his hard gaze lingering on her face.

'Because there was no longer a need. After more than two days in your company it was clear to me that you would make a perfectly reasonable wife. In some areas, more than reasonable.' Thick, dark lashes lowered fractionally and he regarded her with a lazy, slumberous expression in his dark eyes that ignited the dormant flame deep in her pelvis.

'Oh.' Trapped by the raw sexuality in his gaze, she was immediately transported back to the night they'd spent in the cave, and she felt her cheeks flush with embarrassment as she remembered the intimacies they'd shared. 'We nearly—we could have—'

'Yes.' His voice was deep and brushed across her sensitive nerve-endings. 'We could have. We almost did. The fact that you held back because of your impending marriage was very much to your credit. It is because of that restraint that you are standing here now.'

Alexa stared at him with horror. 'Was it a *test?* That night in the cave—were you testing me?'

'No. The passion between us was genuine, and I don't blame you for the way you reacted. You have obviously had an extremely difficult life. It was natural that you would turn to someone if support was offered.'

Was that all he thought it was—*hero worship with chemistry thrown in?*

She knew so much better.

Over the years there had been plenty of people who had offered support and she'd trusted none of them. Karim had been different.

Which just showed that, despite her experience, her judgement was still fallible.

How did she feel about him now?

She'd thought that she loved Karim, only to discover that the man she loved didn't exist.

Confused and miserable, she took another step away from him. 'I can't forgive you for what you did.'

'I have not asked for your forgiveness. What is there to forgive? You wanted to marry the Sultan and you have married the Sultan. You have achieved your objective.' His tone was cool and unemotional. 'Be grateful.'

Grateful?

At that precise moment the only thing she felt grateful for was the fact that she hadn't revealed the extent of her feelings for him. At least she'd been spared that humiliation. He seemed to think that what had sizzled to life between them in the hot, barren desert was nothing more than passion. And she had no intention of enlightening him. Why would she, when she'd already exposed far too much? 'What happens now?'

'I succeeded in keeping our wedding a private affair, but tonight there is a banquet in your honour that will be attended by many neighbouring heads of state and dignitaries.'

'I don't want to go.' Alexa stood still, numb with shock. 'The way I feel at the moment, I won't be able to sit next to you and make small talk.'

His handsome face hardened. '*You* wanted this marriage.'

'*You deceived me.*'

His dark eyes flashed with anger. 'I am not in the habit of re-peating myself, but I am prepared to make allowances for the fact that you are very upset, so this once I will. As you were presented to me, you were *not* a suitable wife for a sultan. I did what had to be done.'

'So when you kissed me that night in Rovina that was just something that had to be done, too, was it?' Remembering her uninhibited response to him, she burned with humiliation, but he merely shrugged, showing no signs of similar discomfort.

'That night in Rovina it was *you* who kissed *me,* but I no longer blame you for that. The chemistry between us is surpris-ingly strong and that is a good thing. And, now, enough. I have been away for several days and I have work to do before the banquet tonight.'

'I'm not going to the banquet.'

'You are the Sultan's wife and you are expected to fulfil that role.'

Her eyes slid slowly to his. Just how much of the rest of the role was she expected to fulfil?

She'd wanted Karim with a desperation that had shocked her, but now she knew he was the Sultan…

Everything felt different.

'You chose this marriage because you wanted my protection, *habibati,*' he said softly. 'You now have that protection. In time I will help you tackle the problems facing Rovina. In return I ex-pect your loyalty and respect.'

'Neither of those can be bought,' she said stiffly. 'I'll attend your banquet because it's my job.' She'd expected her words to anger him, but if anything he seemed mildly amused by her small defiance.

'Good. And what about the wedding night? Are you going to regard that as a job also?'

Her face flamed. 'I have no intention of sleeping with you.' Her impulsive declaration was an attempt to regain some control—a flimsy gesture of self-defence—and he obviously realized that, because he smiled.

'Fiery Alexa. Perhaps you are "the rebel princess," after all. Don't pretend that you feel nothing for me, *habibati,* because we both know that that isn't the case.' He reached out a hand and gently fingered a strand of hair that had escaped from the elaborate twist at the back of her head. 'Those hot desert nights didn't lie.'

'But *you* did! I trusted you, Karim, and you *lied.* And that matters. For a woman, sex is about so much more than chemistry. I trusted the man I was in the desert with.'

'And I am that same man. What is the problem?'

'You're not the same man, Karim! You're someone I don't know.'

'Then I will allow you to know me better. The mystery of who I really am will be solved, tonight, when you come to my bed.' His fingers brushed her cheek in a gesture that was unmistakably possessive, and it took all her will-power to jerk her head away from that dangerously seductive caress.

'Don't touch me.'

'I *will* touch you. And you will touch me back,' he predicted, supremely confident in his sexual power. 'You made your choice, Alexa. It was *you* who sought the Sultan's protection. Now you have that protection and everything that it means. I am by your side, day and night, but this time as your Sultan, not as your bodyguard.'

Day and night.

She swallowed, and she saw the dangerous glint in his dark eyes. He was right, of course. She *had* sought his protection. But she was beginning to wonder whether she'd jumped out of the frying pan and straight into the fire.

CHAPTER NINE

THE wedding banquet was a glittering, glamorous affair that involved several-hundred people, all of whom appeared to want time with Karim.

Alexa stood stiffly by his side, accepting the greetings and congratulations that came her way, still furious with Karim, and even more furious with herself for having been so foolish and gullible.

How could she not have known who he was?

Watching him exercise his diplomatic skills, she marvelled at her own stupidity. Why hadn't she realized sooner that he was the Sultan? Now that she knew the truth about his identity, it seemed so obvious. The clues were everywhere—in the way he held himself and in the way he spoke. He was autocratic and confident, utterly sure of himself, as if he'd been making decisions from his cradle. People pressed around him, all eager to capture even a moment of his attention, and suddenly Alexa started to realize the importance and influence wielded by the man she had married.

She stole a glance at his proud, arrogant profile.

In his Sultan's robes, and discussing a broad range of topics from the falling oil price to desert conservation, she found him intimidating.

Listening to the conversations that went on around her, she soon realized that his opinion was being sought on virtually every subject. And his decisions were bold and confident, devoid of doubt, hesitancy or any apparent nerves on his part.

Even when they sat down to eat, the conversation didn't lighten up.

'I am very unsure. It could be a risky investment,' one ambassador ventured when conversation turned to a particular project that was being undertaken in the desert. 'There is no guarantee of success, Your Excellency.'

Clearly undaunted by that gloomy prediction, Karim merely smiled. 'Neither is there a guarantee of failure, Tariq,' he observed mildly. 'Take the risk. Life is no fun without risk.' His gaze flickered to Alexa as he spoke, and she had a feeling that he was including his marriage in that statement.

As his eyes lingered, she felt a tight, tense tingling in her body and almost laughed at herself.

He hadn't wanted her, but she still wanted him.

The fact that she now knew that the Sultan had gone to extreme lengths to personally prevent his marriage to 'the rebel princess' apparently wasn't enough to subdue the curl of awareness in her body.

Did she have no pride?

Why was she still feeling like this when he'd made it perfectly clear that she was the last person in the world that he would have chosen for his bride?

Yes, he'd married her. But only once he'd discovered that her background had been manufactured. Even in her wildest moments she couldn't pretend that this marriage had anything to do with love.

The Sultan needed a wife, and he'd decided that she was good enough to fulfil that role. She ticked the right boxes. There was no more to it than that.

And as for the chemistry that sizzled between them—well, he was obviously an intensely physical man. All that hot passion in the desert had been nothing more than sex. Any gentleness and kindness she'd felt had been no more than wishful thinking on her part.

Seeking distraction, Alexa tried to participate in the conversation that was taking place around her, but as the banquet progressed she could think of nothing but the night ahead. By the time the Sultan finally rose from the table, she was so on edge and her legs were shaking so much that she could barely walk as he led her firmly from the room.

'Is it always like that? You didn't get any peace for the entire banquet.' As the doors to the Sultan's private living quarters closed behind them, Alexa glanced around her, feeling impossibly jumpy.

All evening she'd been aware of him seated next to her. Occasionally she'd felt the brush of his leg against hers, but even that limited physical contact had been sufficient to drive her body to the point where she was ready to explode.

And she'd hated the fact that she could still feel that way, knowing what he'd done.

Apparently oblivious to her inner torment, Karim strolled across the room and poured himself a drink. 'Somewhere back in the mists of time my ancestors decided that the Sultan's wedding feast should be a time for generosity and giving. I believe that the custom had something to do with the sharing of good fortune.' He glanced towards her, a faint smile touching his mouth. 'They apparently believed that the Sultan would be so ecstatic at the prospect of bedding his new wife that he would be willing to say yes to everyone and everything.'

Her heart-rate doubled. 'And did you?'

'Did I say yes to everything?' His smiled widened. 'Not quite, Alexa. But I was quite possibly a little more approachable than usual.'

She didn't find him approachable. She found him intimidating. *And infuriating.* 'You don't have anything to celebrate. This marriage wasn't what you wanted.'

'But it was what you wanted,' he reminded her softly, his dark eyes quizzical. 'You were willing to travel alone and barefoot across the desert to be my bride, Alexa. Have you forgotten that fact? Why are you suddenly looking as though you would like to run out the door?'

Because everything had changed. Since she'd discovered who he was, everything had felt different. 'I was desperate to escape from my uncle,' she said in a stiff voice, and he gave a slow nod.

'Yes, I understand that. And to do so you were prepared to marry a man who you had never met.'

'But now I *have* met you—'

'And the chemistry between us is nothing short of explosive. Were it not for your reluctance to sleep with another man when you were promised to the Sultan, you would be mine already.' His eyes gleamed with sardonic humour. 'Ironic, is it not? Do you want me to dress as a bodyguard and return to the desert with you? Would that help, Alexa?'

The reminder of just how much she'd revealed of herself caused her to retreat both physically and mentally. She'd let her guard down, but she wasn't going to do it again.

No one was going to hurt her again.

She was angry with him—so angry—and she was going to use that anger to protect herself.

'I was afraid. You comforted me.'

'You're suggesting that the fire between us was nothing more than comfort? I don't think so.' He looked thoughtful. 'You were saving yourself for the Sultan, and rightly so. Fortunately for both of us, the wait is finally over.'

His words made the heat explode inside her body. 'You don't want me!'

'It is no secret that this marriage generally would not have been my personal choice.' Karim put the glass down on the table and looked at her thoughtfully. 'But I am fully aware of my duty to Zangrar, and I have now fulfilled at least part of that duty.'

'Part?'

He strolled towards her, his eyes on her face. 'The second part will be fulfilled when you give birth to our first son.'

Her heart was pounding and she took a step backwards. 'It might be a girl.'

'If it is a girl, then she will be much loved. *Stop* running away,' he commanded, the firm movement of his hand around her waist preventing any further thought of retreat. 'You are behaving like a frightened virgin, and it makes no sense. There is no longer any need to deny the passion that we felt in the desert.'

'Karim—'

'Enough talking.' He growled the order against her lips, and his kiss felt like a lightning strike, the hot brand of his mouth preventing any further protest on her part. And, whether or not she would have made that protest, she no longer knew because the excitement that exploded inside her body consumed all rational thought.

Alexa forgot that he had deceived her.

She forgot everything except the way this man made her feel, and that feeling was so enormous that it diminished everything she'd ever felt before.

His fingers slid into her hair, and the erotic caress of his tongue in her mouth made her head spin, and she lifted her hands to his chest for support because dimly she knew that her knees weren't going to hold her for much longer. He must have sensed the effect he had on her, because he picked her up and carried her through to the bedroom where he put her down gently.

He slid his hands down her back in a slow, deliberate caress that suggested ownership and possession, and it was only when her dress slithered to her feet that she realized that he'd undone the zip.

At any other time the smooth movement would have shocked

her, but she was shaking and shivering with need, her insides churning with anticipation as she gazed at him helplessly. With a characteristic lack of self-consciousness, he stripped naked, exposing his hard, male body to her shy gaze. But then he noticed the look in her eyes and paused, his gaze suddenly questioning as he lifted a hand and brushed the backs of his fingers against her burning cheek.

'Nervous, *habibati?*'

Oh, yes, she was nervous. But why? Was it because he was so confident and self-assured and she was in unfamiliar territory? Or was it simply that she understood the enormity of the step that she was about to take? He was demanding that she gave herself to him. Demanding that she make herself still more vulnerable. And she knew that once she'd given her body to this man there would be no going back.

But there never had been any going back, she thought dizzily as he bent his arrogant, dark head and claimed her mouth again in a possessive kiss that branded her as his property. She felt his fingers move over her heated skin, removing the scraps of underwear that was all that stood between her and nakedness. Then the tips of her breasts were brushing against the rough hair of his chest, and she tilted her head back and gave a soft gasp as sensation pierced her low down in her pelvis.

He hadn't actually touched her properly, and yet every nerve-ending in her body was humming in anticipation. And he must have felt it, too, because he powered her back onto the bed, coming down on top of her in a smooth, purposeful movement.

And suddenly the gentleness and the caution were gone.

The desire had been building for hours. Days. His touch was urgent and her response equally frantic.

She wanted him to touch her.

And she wanted to touch him.

Her fingers slid over the smooth muscle of his shoulder, her nails scraping over his skin as she enjoyed the hard maleness of his body. And he reciprocated, his mouth seeking and demanding. He captured an erect, pink nipple in his mouth and she whimpered as hot, heady pleasure shot through her body. He drew her deeper into the warm, sensual heat of his mouth and then transferred his attentions to her other breast until the gnawing hunger deep inside her became a madness that had to be satisfied. Her hips squirmed and shifted against the silken sheets until she felt his hand slide down her body and hold her still.

She was so desperate—so *ready*—that when he finally reached between her legs she cried out his name in a frantic plea. A shaft of moonlight lit the bedroom, but she saw nothing except the blinding flash of light that accompanied her first orgasm. The excitement was so powerful that she thought she was going to pass out, and then she felt his mouth claim hers again as he swallowed her desperate cries. Her senses were swamped, overloaded and she was so shaken by the sensations that gripped her body that she just clung to the sleek, smooth muscle of his shoulders, holding on.

'You are incredible. *So* responsive,' he purred, and it was only his voice that returned her back to earth and to the realization that his fingers were still deep inside her.

'Oh...' Acknowledging that intimacy, her cheeks flushed and she tried to wriggle away from him, but he simply smiled and gently nudged her thighs apart, his dark hair brushing against her sensitized breasts as his tongue trailed a path down her body. He savoured her as a gourmet might savour each mouthful of an exquisite meal, and she gave a gasp of shock as she felt him gently remove his fingers and replace them with the warm, moist flick of his tongue. Horribly self-conscious, Alexa tried to protest, but her body was so consumed by delicious, wicked pleasure that she simply responded to his silent demand that she open wider for him. And he used his tongue and fingers so gently and skillfuly that the heat started to build again, and she writhed with impatience, just *desperate* for more.

'Please.' She arched her hips off the bed. 'Please, Karim—'

He shifted his body over hers in a smooth, athletic movement, pressing her legs apart with an unfaltering, confident movement.

She felt his erection, hot and heavy between her thighs. She felt him touching her intimately, and she tried to move, but he positioned her as he wanted her and thrust hard, taking possession of her damp, trembling, thoroughly willing body with purposeful force.

It was hot, wild and momentarily painful.

Alexa gasped and sank her nails into the sleek flesh of his shoulder in an attempt to counteract the sudden pain, but it faded almost instantly and she was left only with agonizing pleasure.

'Alexa?' Suddenly tense, Karim paused and stared down at her, and the flicker of doubt in his voice warmed her insides. 'Am I your first lover?'

She opened her eyes and looked straight into his. 'Yes.' She spoke the word softly and then slid her arms around his neck and arched against him, showing him with that single movement exactly what it was that she wanted.

Something flickered in the depths of his dark eyes. 'No other man has touched you.'

'No.' Why was he choosing this moment to indulge in conversation when their bodies were screaming for an entirely different type of communication?

He let out a long breath and kissed the corner of her mouth in a surprisingly tender gesture. 'You please me greatly.' After the briefest hesitation he drove into her a second time, but this time with slightly more restraint. Watching her face, he altered his position slightly and the movement of his body became indistinguishable from the movement of hers as she was slowly devoured by the most exquisite pleasure. The sensation built and

built until she hovered on the edge of ecstasy for a few agonizing seconds, and then finally her body finally convulsed around
his and she felt herself tighten around his shaft. She heard him
groan something unintelligible, and then felt the sudden increase
in masculine thrust as he reached his own completion and ground
himself deep inside her.

The explosion left them both spent.

Alexa lay still, shivering with the aftershocks, stunned by the
passion that had consumed them, and utterly drained of energy.

Her insides were filled with a delicious feeling of warmth, and
not just because of the sex, although that had been amazing. It
was because of the physical closeness.

Just as she'd felt that night in the cave, she felt as though he
cared. And she cared about him, too, didn't she?

No matter how frightening that thought was, she cared.

She loved him.

Bodyguard or Sultan, she loved Karim.

Softened by that knowledge, she suddenly just wanted to hold
him and be held, but at that moment he shifted his weight onto
his elbows and rolled off her, leaving her naked and exposed.

Bereft of the contact, Alexa turned towards him, intending to
snuggle into him and show him just how much his skilled touch
had affected her. And then she caught sight of his hard, unsmil-
ing profile and stopped herself.

What was she thinking?

This man had concealed his identity. He'd deceived her, hadn't
he, and then had showed not one flicker of remorse or regret?

He'd been utterly ruthless in achieving his own ends, and
trusting him or revealing how she felt about him would be a
huge mistake.

That wasn't what this relationship was about, was it? It wasn't
about love or caring, and if she started imagining for one moment
that he was thinking all sorts of soppy thoughts then she would

be setting herself up for a major disappointment, and she'd had enough of those to last her the rest of her lifetime.

Bodyguard or Sultan, this man didn't love her.

Her attention was caught by the blue-black shadow of his jaw and the arrogant set of his features as he lay with his eyes closed, recovering his breath.

Now that their bodies were no longer joined, there was no sign of affection—*not in a glance of the eye or a touch of the hand.*

He'd given her more attention when she'd had the nightmare, and acknowledging that harsh truth killed the tender shoots of happiness that had sprung to life inside her.

He didn't care about her, and it was dangerous to pretend that he did.

He'd married her without even revealing his identity, and that was just *awful.* It meant that he was quite happy to lie when it suited him, which made him no different from all the people who had worked for her uncle over the years. The people who had deceived her and put her life at risk.

Karim wasn't interested in her love. He didn't *want* love. He didn't want to share emotion. Perhaps he didn't even *feel* emotion—he certainly never showed it. He was a loner. A man who didn't need others. And the fact that they'd shared hot, steamy passion in the darkness of the night didn't change that fact.

He'd married her because he needed a wife, and once he'd discovered that her rebel background had been fabricated by her uncle she'd been as good a candidate as the next woman. But she wasn't special to him. It could have just as easily been a different woman lying here now. She couldn't afford to forget that. She wasn't going to make the mistake of confusing sexual intimacy with anything deeper. That would only increase the embarrassment for both of them.

The sleek skin of his bronzed shoulder was within tantalizing reach of her fingers, and she curled her hands into fists in order to resist the almost overwhelming temptation to touch. She lay there wondering how it was possible to experience such intimacy and yet feel so very, very alone.

She'd shared herself with this man, emotionally and physically, but he had no feelings for her and was willing to lie and deceive when it suited him.

Yes, she was finally safe from her uncle.

But she'd fallen in love, and that made her more vulnerable than she'd ever been in her life before. Whether he knew it or not, Karim had the ability to cause greater wounds than anything her uncle had ever inflicted.

Karim lay on his back, struggling to recover from the most explosive climax of his life. The intimate recollection of her willing body wrapped around his was all it took to boost his arousal to almost agonizing levels.

Never before in his life could he remember being so turned on by a woman.

Slightly disconcerted by the power of his feelings, he searched for an explanation.

Amazing sex. Was that what was happening here?

Well, yes, obviously. And he wasn't going to pretend that her sexual innocence hadn't added an extra dimension to their relationship, because clearly it had. The fact that she had been a virgin had satisfied an elemental masculine part of himself, and confirmed that he'd been absolutely right in his choice of wife.

And suddenly he felt remarkably genial towards her.

Normally by now he would have left the bed and distanced himself from the snuggling and demonstrative outpourings that inevitably followed sex, but what was the point of that? He *knew* that Alexa had feelings for him. It would be only fair for her to be allowed to show them. This was not a one-night stand—they were now married.

Karim lay still, waiting for the feeling of panic that had always accompanied the mere thought of the word *relationship,* but nothing happened. He just felt replete and satisfied, and more than ready to haul her underneath him and repeat the entire performance.

Wondering why she was holding back when he was willing to tolerate and possibly welcome her affection, he turned towards her, and it came as a shock to discover that, far from holding herself poised to embrace him, his bride had actually fallen asleep.

Karim stilled, his brooding features locked in an a expression of astounded disbelief as he studied the slumbering woman by his side.

He'd never before known a woman to just fall asleep after sex.

He frowned slightly, his eyes lingering on the softness of her mouth and the gentle flush of her cheeks. The knowledge that *he* was responsible for that flush sent a wave of instantaneous lust tearing through his body, and he was seriously tempted to wake her up just so that he could set about exhausting her one more time.

Their love-making had been exceptionally energetic and passionate, he conceded, stroking a wisp of hair away from her face with a gentle hand. Perhaps it wasn't altogether surprising that she'd fallen asleep immediately, even thought it meant that she hadn't had the chance to express how she felt about him. All the same, it was unusual that she hadn't chosen to drape herself over him before falling asleep. There was something about the female sex that made them need to cling, especially after sex.

But Alexa wasn't clinging. In fact, she wasn't touching him at all.

Studying the fragile, vulnerable woman curled up by his side, Karim felt a sudden burst of explosive anger towards her uncle. She was probably just afraid to trust him. After all, her uncle had made her life hell.

A fierce desire to protect her from any more stress surged through him, and he sucked in a breath, spooked by the intensity of that feeling, and almost immediately reassuring himself that nothing could be more natural than a man wanting to protect his wife. All the same, the irony of the situation didn't escape him. He'd always made it a personal rule not to spend the entire night with a woman, because he'd learned at a young age that they just couldn't separate the physical from the emotional. After sex they just wanted to cling. And here he was, finally willing to allow a woman to cling, and she was too tired to take advantage of his generosity. They could have parked a car in the gap between them in the bed.

Absorbing another possibility for her behaviour—*that she could have been afraid to tell him how she felt*—Karim lay back against the pillows, vowing that once she awoke he was going to encourage her to say all the things that she was clearly holding back.

Alexa opened her eyes to find sunshine lighting the room and Karim watching her. He was just so masculine, she thought dizzily, as her eyes rested on his dark jaw and then lifted to his molten, dark eyes. He acknowledged her scrutiny with lazy, almost sleepy amusement. He was ridiculously, impossibly sexy, and she just wanted to melt against him and beg him to repeat what he'd done to her the night before.

Weakened by the memory, she dragged her eyes away from his, but they merely settled lower on his body and she felt hot colour ooze into her cheeks.

He'd deceived her.

He knew how much it had taken for her to give him her trust, and he'd abused that trust by not telling her the truth. And he'd shown no regret or remorse. In fact, he'd made it clear that the subject was closed.

'How are you feeling?' His tone was soft and encouraging, and connected straight to her insides.

Horribly vulnerable? 'Fine.' As she delivered this minimal response, his eyes narrowed.

'Fine?' Clearly, he'd been expecting to hear something different.

'How are *you* feeling?'

'Generous. You are the most incredible lover, *habibati.*'

The look in his eyes made her forget for a moment that she was angry and hurt. 'Oh.'

'Last night you fell asleep.' His hand rested on her hip and then gently slid down her thigh in a seductive movement that had every nerve-ending in her body tingling.

'I was feeling tired.'

'And I think perhaps you were feeling very shy,' he purred, this time stroking his hand over the soft curve of her bottom. 'I'm sure there were things you wanted to say, and I want you to know that I am prepared to hear whatever it is. You're my wife. I don't want you to hold back. Honesty is important.'

'Really?' That wasn't what his comments the day before had led her to believe, but she was oddly relieved that he was prepared to allow her to talk about how she felt. 'I'm surprised to hear you say that—but if that's the case then you should know that I still think what you did was completely wrong.'

'Wrong?' His body tensed and he repeated the word as if he'd never heard it before, his eyes shimmering with raw incredulity. 'What, precisely, was *wrong?* You were *incredibly* turned on.'

Mortified by that less than subtle reminder of her own feverish response, Alexa drew away from him slightly. 'I was not talking about the sex! I was talking about the fact that you didn't tell me who you were! That was what was *wrong,* Karim. I trusted you, and you took advantage of that trust. I told you everything about myself and you told me *nothing* about you.'

He muttered something that she didn't understand and then

sprang from the bed, apparently indifferent to the fact that he was naked. 'Why do you persist in sulking about something that is now in the past?'

She sat up in bed. 'I'm *not* sulking, and you were the one who said that you wanted me to say whatever I was feeling.' Lacking his confidence, she clutched the sheet against her naked body. 'I've just told you how I'm feeling!'

Karim prowled across the room like a caged beast, and then turned back towards her with something approaching a growl. 'I was not expecting you to use the opportunity to simply rehash an old conflict which should now be in the past!'

'So I'm allowed to speak as long as I say what you want to hear, is that right?' She was trembling with frustration. The fact that he *still* didn't see the need to apologize for his deception somehow made the situation worse. He obviously couldn't see that he'd done anything wrong. 'It isn't in the past for me! You deceived me, Karim. You concealed your identity.'

'And with good reason. My only objective was to find a way out of marrying "the rebel princess."'

'But that wasn't who I was.'

'I know that *now.*' His tone was grim. 'But I did *not* know it until I spent time with you. All I had in front of me was a long list of your extravagances and risk-taking behaviour. The people of Zangrar deserved better after everything they suffered at the hands of my stepmother.'

It was the first time he'd revealed anything remotely personal about his family, and his statement momentarily distracted her from her anger. 'What has your stepmother got to do with this?'

He tensed, and his expression was cold and discouraging. 'Everything. But that is none of your business.'

'I disagree! If I'm being blamed for her misdeeds, then I at least deserve to hear about what she did.'

Karim strode across to the window and paused for a moment.

Then he turned back to face her, his face set in hard, uncompromising lines. 'When my mother died, my father naturally became a target for no end of unscrupulous women.' He gave a cynical smile. 'That's the way the world works, isn't it? Where there is money and power, there will always be women. Unfortunately women, especially beautiful women, were my father's weakness.'

'Oh.'

'Yes, oh.' A muscle worked in his lean jaw. 'My stepmother created havoc. She managed to drag huge sums of money from my father, and spent it all on herself. She thought only of glamour and parties, and had no interest whatsoever in improving life for the people of Zangrar. She was the original rebel princess. Her thoughtless, selfish behaviour caused much unrest.'

'I can imagine.' Hadn't William done much the same to the people of Rovina? 'Didn't you have any influence with your father?'

'She made sure that I didn't. She persuaded my father to send me to boarding school from the age of seven.' He gave a hard smile. 'From there I went to university to study law, and then into the army. At that point I was back in Zangrar for long periods, but often working undercover in the desert. During that time I learned a great deal about what the people thought about my stepmother and also my father.'

'She didn't have children of her own?'

'That would have required caring about someone else other than herself, and she was not the type to share the limelight. As I grew up I saw the effect she was having on Zangrar but was unable to change what was happening. From the army I went to business school, and then I returned to Zangrar, ready to take up a senior post in government and try to curb the behaviour of my stepmother.'

Alexa studied him for a moment, knowing that he would be a formidable adversary. 'You succeeded?'

'He was completely addicted to her, able to see her faults

but unable to resist her. And she was a clever woman. She used every trick in the book to get me on her side.' He caught her glance and gave a wry smile. 'Yes, even that one, but it didn't work, of course. My father's experience had taught me at a young age to be wary of women, especially women like her. Things were fraught, to say the least—' He broke off and Alexa found that she was holding her breath, waiting for the rest of the story.

'And?'

'She was killed in a fall from a horse. My father was devastated, and had a heart attack a few days later. Zangrar was in chaos, but I was optimistic that I would be able to bring things under control and restore the confidence of the people.' He paused and his mouth hardened. 'And then I discovered that my father had, years before, arranged my marriage to another rebel princess, a matter he'd omitted to reveal before his death. I knew that if the marriage went ahead all the good work would be undone. It was the only way of protecting Zangrar.'

Alexa stared at him, her anger fizzling out like a firework doused by a bucket of water. 'I—I didn't know any of that.'

'Well, you know now. Remember it before you fling accusations of deceit in my direction.'

The hardness of his tone sent a chill through her insides. It was hard to believe that this was the same man who had made love to her so passionately the night before. 'I'm not a mind reader, Karim! You should have told me this before.'

'It wasn't relevant.'

'It was to me! It would have helped me understand you!'

'I have never expected or required a woman to understand me.'

Alexa stared at him helplessly. All her preconceived ideas about him had melted away, and now she just felt confused. 'What is it that you want from me? You said that you wanted me to be honest, so I have been honest, and now you're angry. What was it that you expected me to say when I woke up this morning?'

'I *expected* you to show affection!'

His words were so surprising that for a moment she just gaped at him. 'Affection?'

'When we were in the desert, you were happy to show your feelings for me. You clung to me and told me how desperate you were for someone to just hold you and tell you that everything was going to be all right.'

Reminded of her unguarded declaration, Alexa coloured and shook her head. 'I didn't—'

'No!' His tone was hard and he raised a hand to silence her. 'I won't allow you to deny *or* retreat from those feelings, Alexa! Your ability to show your feelings was one of the reasons I decided you would make a suitable wife. I did *not* want to be with a woman like my stepmother, who had no feelings for anyone other than herself. I didn't want that for myself or for our children.'

Their children? Swept along on a tide of a conversation that was entirely unexpected, Alexa froze, suddenly feeling incredibly vulnerable. Had he really guessed how she felt about him? 'I didn't have feelings for *you,* I had feelings for my bodyguard. You made me feel safe—that's all it was.' The need to protect herself was so ingrained that she didn't even think about it. 'And what you saw was gratitude, Karim, and I can't believe that someone as experienced as you would mistake gratitude for something deeper.'

It suddenly seemed desperately important that he didn't know just how much of herself she'd given to him. 'You helped me escape from my uncle. You could have been a flea-bitten camel with three legs and I still would have felt grateful to you.'

He lifted one dark eyebrow. 'You expect me to believe that it was gratitude that made you cling to me when you had a bad dream? Gratitude that made you hold on to me in the cave?'

'Of course.' *What did he want from her?*

Did he really expect her to drop her heart at his feet just so that he could tread on it a second time? No way! As far as she was concerned, she'd already given away far too much about how she felt, and had no intention of exposing any more of herself. 'You might be the Sultan, but you can't just order someone to care for you. Affection has to be earned, Karim. Even by sultans.'

'I rescued you from your uncle. I married you, which is what you wanted. Just how high is the price for your affection, Alexa?'

Extremely high. 'Why would you *want* me to have feelings for you, anyway? You told me that you don't do love.'

'You're my wife.' He spoke with lethal emphasis and there was no missing the possessive note to his voice. 'You have feelings for me, I know you have. I expect you to express them, as you did that night in the cave. I want you to be honest with me, otherwise this marriage won't be a happy one.'

Having delivered that depressing prediction, he turned sharply and strode into the bathroom, slamming the door with such force that she flinched.

Alexa collapsed back against the soft pillows, feeling completely shattered by the confrontation.

He wanted her to be truthful with him, and yet when before this moment had *he* been honest with *her*? He'd allowed her to make her wedding vows before revealing his true identity. *What sort of honesty was that?*

On the other hand, he clearly had no reason at all to trust women, she thought miserably, and everything he'd just told her about his stepmother did explain a great deal about the way he'd behaved.

But it didn't make her any more inclined to reveal her feelings.

She covered her face with her hands, exasperated with herself. *What was there to reveal that he hadn't already guessed?* Clearly he already knew *exactly* how she felt.

And that was the problem, wasn't it?

Love had made her vulnerable in a way that she'd never been

vulnerable before, and she was desperately looking for ways to protect herself.

Yes, they were married, but that didn't mean that she had to give him everything he was asking of her.

Alexa lay there listening to the sounds of the shower, more confused than ever before. The closed bathroom door suddenly seemed symbolic of their marriage.

There was a barrier between them.

The question was, could it be moved?

CHAPTER TEN

KARIM stood under the icy jets of the shower, ignoring the painful throb in his injured arm as he waited for the anger and frustration to fade.

Talk about making a guy jump through hoops.

Did she have any idea how many women had dreamed of lying where she was lying now? And yet, instead of showing the affection that he *knew* she felt, she was obviously still sulking about the fact that he hadn't revealed who he was.

Why was she so reluctant to show her feelings when she was now safe and had no reason to hide?

He allowed the water to stream over his hair and his body as he considered the more disturbing question.

Why did he care?

Since when had he ever demanded affection from a woman before? Never. Usually he was leaping out of bed to avoid any expression of that exact emotion.

'Why are you taking a cold shower?' A faltering female voice cut through his thoughts, and he opened his eyes and dragged a hand over his face to clear his vision.

Alexa stood in front of him. She was wearing his robe, and the fact that it was much too big for her just made her look more fragile than ever. Her amazing bright red-gold hair tumbled over her shoulders, and the expression in her blue eyes was uncertain. She looked like a woman who wasn't at all sure of her welcome.

'I came to apologize.' Her voice was stiff and formal. 'I—I didn't know anything about your stepmother before today. Obviously, I understand now why you wanted to avoid marrying me at all costs.'

Karim reached out and stopped the flow of water with an abrupt thump of his hand. 'Another "rebel princess" was the last thing that Zangrar needed.'

She gave a painful smile. 'Yes, I can see that. I just wish you'd trusted me with the information before, but you didn't, did you? Not even when you knew the truth about me.'

'I'm not accustomed to trusting anyone.'

'And neither am I.' She pulled the robe more firmly around her, as if afraid that it might somehow fall apart, and he noted the gesture with narrowed eyes.

She was always protecting herself. Physically, emotionally.

'You trusted me enough to marry me, Alexa.'

'I had to. You were my last hope.' She hesitated. 'You have to understand something about my life before you judge me too harshly. You're expecting me to reveal everything about myself, but you're forgetting that I've spent the last sixteen years not allowing myself to do that. It's how I stayed alive.'

'I know.' He reached for a towel and knotted it around his waist. 'But you're safe now. Do you believe that?'

'Yes, but I can't change overnight.'

'I expect you to be honest with me.'

'You're expecting me to reveal everything about myself, but you don't do the same thing, do you?'

'I have already delivered what you expected of this marriage. Protection. It was never a part of our deal that I spill my guts.'

She flinched. 'You're right, I *was* the one who insisted on this marriage, and you *did* rescue me from my uncle. I owe you a great deal, I know that. And I'm prepared to be everything a sultan's wife should be—I just didn't expect that to include affection.' She sounded confused and almost humble. 'You took me by surprise. No one has ever wanted that from me before. I didn't know *you* wanted that from me.'

Until last night he hadn't known he wanted it either.

'You're my wife. I want everything from you, Alexa.'

It took her a moment to answer, and she kept her eyes fixed somewhere in the vicinity of his injured arm. 'I'm not used to trusting anyone. I'm not sure that I can do it.' She drew a breath. 'It's scary.'

'Scary?' His own anger and frustration died in the face of that shaky confession. 'From what I can gather, your life has been at risk since you were a child. You've shown astonishing bravery. How can showing affection terrify you?'

'Because I've discovered that trusting someone and then watching them reject you is the most agonizing experience of all.' Looking desperately vulnerable, she took a step backwards, and almost tripped over the trailing hem of his dressing gown.

His hands shot out and prevented her fall. Raw excitement exploded through his body, and he released her as if he'd been burnt. He didn't understand the way he reacted to this woman. When he was close to her he lost all grip on control.

Like his father?

Unsettled by that possibility, it was Karim's turn to take a step backwards. 'You're talking about your uncle?'

'No. I never trusted him. But in the beginning there were others.' She swallowed painfully. 'I was so young, Karim. Just a child. And I was used to being loved. I'd been loved by my parents, and for a while I just turned to everyone, hoping that someone would help me.'

Karim felt something tighten inside him. 'And no one did?'

'They were all too afraid of my uncle. But I was *so* desperate for support that it took me a long time to stop trusting. I suppose part of me just didn't want to believe that this was happening to me. It's been such a long time since I've trusted and showed affection; I'm not sure I can just switch it on again that easily.'

'You can and you will, because you have no need to be afraid now.' His voice harsh, Karim gave in to the impulse and reached for her, pulling her against him. '*No one* will touch you again and, despite what you think, you *can* trust me.'

'Can I?' She looked up at him, her blue eyes wide and vulnerable.

An unfamiliar emotion stirred inside him as he swiftly volunteered the reassurance she was seeking. 'Yes. Everything I said to you that night in the cave still stands. I will not allow anyone or anything to hurt you.'

'Because I'm your wife.' There was a wistful note in her tone that connected straight to his internal alarm-system.

'Of course.' *What did she want from him?*

'Y-you said our marriage might not be happy.'

'I said it wouldn't be if you hold back. Be honest with me, Alexa, and we will do very well together.'

'Will we? But you don't do love, do you, Karim? You've already told me that.'

He could have lied, but he decided that there had already been enough of that between them. 'I've said that you can trust me. I will never let you down as your uncle did. I needed a wife, you need protection. It is a fair exchange.' Deciding that they'd done far too much talking for one day, Karim parted the edges of the robe and allowed it to slide from her shoulders. 'This is much, *much* too big for you.'

'Oh.' Standing in front of him naked, she blushed a shade of hot pink, and he felt a thud of instantaneous arousal at the sight of her smooth, creamy skin.

'You are incredibly beautiful, have I told you that this morning?'

'No.' She sounded oddly insecure, and didn't look at him, her eyes instead focused on some point in the corner of his bathroom. 'Does your arm hurt?'

'Not at all,' he lied, sliding his hand under her chin and forcing her to look at him.

'What is it you want from me, Karim?'

Reminding himself that actions spoke louder than words, he curved her lush, naked body against his. 'Everything,' he muttered against her mouth, and then groaned as he felt her full breasts brush against his chest. 'Everything, Alexa. Remember that.'

She felt so good.

Suddenly kissing wasn't enough, and he caught her up in his arms and carried her back through to the bedroom, where he spread her flat and came down on top of her in a decisive movement designed to prevent any second thoughts on her part.

By the time he'd finished with her she wouldn't be able to prevent herself from showing her feelings, he vowed to himself as he brought his mouth down on hers, and prepared to convert her from shy bride to quivering, adoring female.

The sweetness of her lips sent a vicious punch through his body, and he was about to abandon foreplay and just move straight on to the main event when he remembered just how inexperienced she was.

He did *not* want to hurt her.

So he reined in his natural instincts and instead set about seducing his new wife with every skill he knew. Using hands and mouth, he explored every inch of her trembling, writhing body until it was difficult to know who was the more desperate.

'Karim...' She sobbed his name and pressed her hips against him in blatant invitation but he ignored his own urgent desire and the plea in her voice, and instead continued to drive her wild.

'Karim! Please, please...' She twisted and shifted in an agony of sexual excitement, and he lowered himself over her and slid his hand to the moist juncture of her thighs. She was so hot and wet and ready for him that he had to grit his teeth to prevent himself from taking her hard and fast.

Instead he entered her slowly, his muscles rippling with the effort of holding back, and as her silken warmth closed around him he groaned aloud and buried his face in her neck, breathing in her scent and tasting her skin with his mouth.

And then he felt the first spasms of her orgasm tighten around him like a fist, and he lost all control and drove into her with all the passion and urgency that her body was demanding. Karim slammed headlong into a climax of such explosive proportions that his vision blurred and his mind went totally blank. She felt hot, so *hot,* and he thrust and thrust, drinking in her cries of agonized pleasure, feeling the slick slide of her skin against his as they raised the temperature of the atmosphere from comfortable to steamy.

It was so intense and consuming that a considerable time passed before he was able to regard himself as a human being with a brain.

As the spasms in his body faded and his thought processes gradually reawoke, Karim pressed a lingering kiss on the damp skin at the base of her throat.

So much for restraint, he thought dryly, relieving her of his weight and closing his eyes in an attempt to recover some of his control. And then he felt her roll towards him, and he turned his head to look at her.

Her hair was wildly tangled, her cheeks flushed and her lips softly swollen from his kisses. She looked like a woman who had been well and truly loved, and he was just about to pull her on top of him and teach her an entirely new position when she tentatively placed a hand on his abdomen and snuggled against him.

Karim tensed and then gave a satisfied smile and curled an arm around her, drawing her closer, providing the encouragement she so clearly needed. 'That was amazing, *habibati,*' he said huskily, and gave a satisfied smile as he felt her relax against him.

'Yes.' She spoke so softly that for a moment he wondered if he'd imagined it. Her fingers moved softly, tentatively, across his heated skin as if she was checking that he was real. 'Will it be all right, Karim?'

Knowing just how independent she was, he felt a sudden surge of emotion at this unexpected plea for reassurance. 'Of course.' He tightened his hold on her. 'You're mine now.'

A month later, Alexa couldn't believe how much her life had changed.

For the first time in her life, she felt safe.

There were armed guards everywhere in the palace, and security within the walls of the Citadel was so high that she felt herself gradually relax, soothed by the knowledge that she was finally safe from her uncle. And the ability to walk through sun-filled courtyards without once glancing over her shoulder, and climb into a car without first checking the brakes, felt amazing.

She explored Zangrar, made a concerted effort to learn the language, and then practised it with everyone she met. Sometimes Karim joined her, but the demands on his time were endless and occasionally she had to wait until the evening to spend time with him.

'I feel as though I should make an appointment to see you,' she told him one evening as they ate dinner together in one of the many sunny courtyards that lay within the palace walls.

'You missed me?' Karim leaned back in his chair, his dark eyes teasing. 'That is good to know, *habibati*. I was told that you visited the hospital today. That was generous of you.'

'They showed me round and described all the work they are doing.' Alexa chewed her lip for a moment, and then took a deep breath, unsure as to how her request would be received. 'They need a new MRI scanner, Karim. The head of the radiology department was telling me everything they could do if they had one. Do you think—I mean, I said I'd mention it...' She broke off, and he raised a dark eyebrow, his expression amused.

'You have been spending my money again, Alexa?'

She blushed. 'I promised I'd ask you, that's all.'

With a casual flick of his hand, he dismissed the hovering staff, his eyes never leaving her face. 'The citizens of Zangrar are clearly beginning to learn that the Sultan can deny his wife nothing.' The warmth of his gaze made her blush deepen.

As time passed, she simply wanted him more, not less.

'So—you'll let them have the scanner? I really think they need one.'

He studied her face thoughtfully. 'If you think it, then it will be done. I will direct Omar to deal with it.'

'You will? Really?' Touched that he trusted her judgement, she smiled at him. 'Thank you.'

'What next? Whose life do you want to improve?' He leaned back in his chair, clearly enjoying the conversation. 'Just be careful that you don't become a soft touch, Alexa.'

'It feels good, doesn't it, being able to help?' Alexa's smile faded, and she swallowed back the lump that had suddenly appeared in her throat. 'That's how my father was. It didn't matter how big the request, if he believed that it was right and that it would help Rovina then he would move mountains to make it happen. Everyone loved him. He just cared, you know? He put everyone else first, always.'

'Clearly the spirit of the father lives on in the daughter,' Karim said softly, leaning across the table and taking her hand. 'He would be proud of you, Alexa.'

'No.' She shook her head, feeling despair wash over her. 'What have I ever done for Rovina? I've just watched while William destroyed everything that my father built.'

'You were a child. You had no one, and yet somehow you

managed to stay alive. And you managed to remain brave and honest when people all around you were corrupt.' The Sultan's tone was suddenly hard. 'He will be punished, Alexandra. You can count on it.'

His words startled her. It hadn't occurred to her that he would deal with William. 'You're planning to confront him? You have a plan?'

Karim released her hand and rose to his feet. 'This is not a subject for discussion.'

'But if it involves Rovina—'

'Alexa—' He turned to face her and his expression was forbidding. 'You swore to trust me.'

'I do trust you, but—'

'Then do not question me on this matter. When the time is right I will tell you more. For now, I just require that you stay within the walls of the Citadel. Do you promise me that?'

'Yes, but—'

'Always with you there is a "but".' Clearly torn between exasperation and amusement, he pulled her into his arms. 'And I have learned that when that is the case there is only one effective way to silence you.'

As he swung her up into his arms and kissed her hard, Alexa forgot the point of the conversation. It was always like this. When she was with him, her mind ceased to work.

And during the days that followed she couldn't quite work out why she wasn't completely happy.

This was her dream, wasn't it? Marriage to a powerful sultan who could offer her the protection that she'd never enjoyed before. In fact, it was better than any dream, because never once had it crossed her mind that she might fall in love with the powerful man who was now her husband.

Life was good.

Instead of hiding herself away and being suspicious of everyone, she walked about freely and enjoyed the attentiveness of the Sultan's enormous number of staff.

There was really only one thing missing.

Love.

Karim didn't love her.

In the bedroom he was flatteringly attentive. Every single night without fail, and frequently during the day, as well, he dragged every last bit of response from her shivering, aching body, and she held nothing back because she no longer knew how to.

And it wasn't just in the bedroom that he seemed determined to impress her.

He also made an effort to be thoughtful in other areas, and she was incredibly touched—not by the jewellery or the extravagant gifts that arrived for her on a daily basis, but by the smaller, thoughtful gestures that showed that he'd given real thought to pleasing her. Having discovered her interest in history, he had insisted on taking her on a tour of the medieval Citadel, showing her the narrow passageways, the hidden souks and the ancient temples that had been built by his ancestors.

Karim seemed determined to introduce her to every facet of Zangrar, and Alexa accepted enthusiastically, glad of anything which took her mind off the more personal side of their relationship.

As the Sultan's wife she wanted to fit in.

And, as time passed and she heard more about the reprehensible behaviour of his stepmother, she was more and more determined to make Karim proud of her, and determined to do for Zangrar what she had been denied in her beloved Rovina.

Perhaps in time he might grow to love her, she thought wistfully as she sat in the shade one afternoon, watching a bubbling fountain in one of the many peaceful enclosed gardens that lay within the palace walls.

Hearing someone calling her name, she glanced up and noticed Omar, Karim's chief advisor hurrying towards her across the grass. 'Omar?' Forgetting her discarded shoes, Alexa scrambled to her feet and brushed the grass from her dress. 'Is something the matter?'

'There has been a most terrible accident, Your Highness.'

'The Sultan is injured?' Horrified, Alexa took a step towards him, but he lifted a hand to reassure her and shook his head quickly.

'His Excellency is safe and well,' Omar said hastily. 'But we have received a report of an explosion at one of the oil fields. No one seems to know how serious it is. His Excellency sends his apologies to you. As you know he is presently out of the country, attending a delegation in Kazban, and he was due home this evening. But arrangements are being made to fly him directly to the accident site. He wished me to inform you that he will be in touch as soon as he can.'

'But presumably it will take him ages to reach the site if he's coming from Kazban?'

'That fact is regrettable, but unavoidable.'

'But someone needs to be there to help. To make sure that everything that can be done is being done.' Slipping her feet into her shoes, Alexa made an immediate decision. 'I will go, Omar. I will visit and see how we can help. In that way I can be ready to inform Karim when he arrives.'

Omar stared at her in consternation. 'That would not be fitting, Your Highness.'

'Why not?'

'The last Sultan's wife would not have dreamed of acting in such a way.'

'But I'm not the last Sultan's wife,' Alexa pointed out gently. 'I'm *this* Sultan's wife, and I want to help. I am not some useless wallflower, Omar.'

'But—'

'The Sultan married me because he discovered that I was not like his stepmother, isn't that right?'

Omar inhaled sharply. 'Yes, Your Highness, but—'

'So I would be very grateful if you would arrange a flight for me. How far is this place?'

'Half an hour by helicopter, but His Excellency gave strict instructions that you were not to leave the Citadel.'

'He was being overprotective.' And that knowledge warmed her whole body. 'That danger no longer exists.'

'But—'

'Arrange it, Omar.' Alexa picked up her hat and walked quickly towards the palace. 'I'll just go and change into something more suitable.'

'My wife has flown to the oil field?' Karim's eyes glittered dangerously as he spoke on the phone to his chief advisor. 'And you allowed this?'

The phone crackled. 'She was most insistent, and your wife is *not* an easy woman to dissuade, Your Excellency.'

'Nevertheless, you *should* have dissuaded her. I gave instructions that she should remain within the walls of the Citadel.' Feeling a stab of fear, Karim sucked in a breath. 'Tell me you sent guards with her.'

'Two of them, Your Excellency.'

All the same.

Suddenly a suspicion entered his brain, and that suspicion swiftly changed to cold dread. Could her uncle be behind the explosion? 'Phone through to the helicopter, Omar. I don't want her to land at the oil field. It isn't safe.'

'It's too late. They landed half an hour ago, Your Excellency. Her Royal Highness is already tending the injured.'

And, knowing Alexandra, she wasn't looking over her shoulder.

Karim felt a sudden rush of tension.

And that was his fault, wasn't it?

He'd insisted that she trust. He'd encouraged her to open up and give more and more of herself to him. But, in doing so, he had unwittingly put her in danger.

She no longer wore the cloak of suspicion that had kept her alive for so long.

She no longer believed that her uncle was a threat, and he hadn't wanted to disturb her shiny new happiness by telling her the truth: *that the threat against her life was as real as ever.*

Karim stared out of the window, battling with a feeling of helplessness that was entirely new to him. Never had he felt so desperately afraid and out of control of a situation. 'Omar.' Watching as the desert flashed by beneath him, he spoke into the phone again. 'I want you to contact the bodyguards. Anyone. You must get a message through to Alexa. Tell her to leave. Immediately. Tell her to get out of there.' *While she still could...*

'I'll do my best, Your Excellency.'

Karim's jaw tightened as he cut the connection. He would arrive at the oil field in fifteen minutes. The question was, would he be too late?

Alexa worked alongside the paramedics, treating the casualties and helping with the rescue mission. It was hot, filthy work and she had just applied a bandage to another bleeding wound when a man hurried towards her.

'There is someone injured in the control room,' he said breathlessly. 'You are needed.'

'Of course.' Without hesitating, she rose to her feet and followed, wiping her dirty, grimy hands on her trousers.

It could have been worse, she told herself. The drilling equipment was damaged and some of the injuries were severe, but there was no loss of life. Karim wouldn't care about the economic implications, she knew that, but he *would* care about the people.

Hoping that the man in the control room wasn't seriously hurt, Alexa hurried up the steps and pushed open the door. He was lying on the floor, a dark stain slowly spreading across his jacket. 'Call the paramedics…' She turned to the man who had led her there, but he had gone and in his place stood her uncle.

'Well, well.' His eyes slid over her dusty, blood-stained clothes. 'Life as the Sultan's wife is clearly nowhere near as glamorous as you'd anticipated.'

Alexa was so shocked to see him that she just stood staring in horror, unable to speak or think clearly.

Her uncle?

Her uncle was here in Zangrar?

The man on the floor groaned in agony, and Alexa turned, her response to his distress instinctive.

'Don't move, Alexandra.' William's tone was deadly, and her gaze flickered to the injured man and then back to her uncle.

'He needs help.'

William shrugged. 'We don't always get what we deserve.'

Anger mingled with the fear. 'What are you doing here?'

'Claiming what is mine.' He gave a nasty smile. 'And you were always mine, Alexa.'

She felt her heart-rate double and her palms grow damp. 'I have bodyguards outside.'

'Unfortunately for you, they were called away.' William pushed the door shut, turned the key with a deliberate movement and then walked towards her. 'You got lucky so many times, Alexandra. You were the original cat with nine lives. But those lives are all used up now, and there is no one here to save you. It's just you and me. You're not going to be blowing out the candles on your next birthday cake, Alexa.'

The injured man on the floor groaned again, and Alexa bit her lip. 'Please—let me just help him and then I'll go with you, if that is what you want.'

'You're not going anywhere.' William's voice was calm as he withdrew the gun from his pocket. 'You thought the Sultan was going to save you, but you're going to die right here in the desert, along with the snakes and the scorpions. It's long overdue. You should have died with your parents.'

Alexa stared at the gun. 'I never did you harm.'

'You ruined everything I worked for.' The calm left and his tone was vicious. 'I was the Regent, but I was never given the respect I was owed. After your parents' death, all the country cared about was you. The little orphan princess. You really knew how to earn the sympathy vote, didn't you, Alexa?'

Alexa licked dry lips. 'William—'

'Everyone fell in love with you. And that couldn't work, don't you see that? I couldn't allow you to live, knowing that people were all looking towards the day when you would become Queen. You had to have an accident.' William giggled hysterically, and the gun shook in his hand. 'But you were incredibly hard to kill. I had to become more and more inventive.'

Alexa could hardly breathe. She couldn't believe she'd put herself in this situation. 'Killing me will achieve nothing.'

'On the contrary, it will give me great satisfaction. They've taken my throne, do you know that? The Council.' His tone a vicious growl, William pointed the gun at her head. 'They've forced me to step aside. They want you to step into my place. And that isn't going to happen.'

Out of the corner of her eye, Alexa saw movement at the door and the window. Maybe if she could just keep him talking for a moment longer…

'I'm sure it's all just a misunderstanding.'

'Maybe.' His smile was ugly. 'But it will all be cleared up when you are dead. Those guys were meant to finish you off in the desert, but your overzealous bodyguard got in the way.'

Alexa saw his finger move on the gun and flung herself to one side, and at the same time there was a loud crash and the sound of breaking glass as Karim burst through the door along with several bodyguards.

In one smooth, determined movement he disarmed her uncle and punched him so hard that William staggered into the desk behind him and then collapsed to the floor, stunned by the blow.

Without pausing, Karim bent down and yanked him back onto his feet, this time slamming him against the wall with propulsive force, the expression on his face so cold and frightening that for the first time in her life Alexa saw fear in her uncle's eyes.

Karim tightened strong fingers around William's throat, his voice thickened by anger. 'You will never, *ever,* lay a finger on my wife again. Nor will you say a single demeaning word about her in private or in public.' William struggled weakly and started to gasp for air, but Karim didn't release his hold. 'For sixteen years she endured your relentless persecution and she was totally alone. It ends now. *It finishes here!*'

Seeing her uncle's eyes bulge, Alexa struggled to her feet. 'Karim—' But her voice was no more than a whisper, and the Sultan didn't hear her.

He was blind with anger and all his focus was on her uncle. 'She isn't alone any more. She's mine, and she has me to protect her.'

'Karim!' Alexa tried again, her voice louder this time. 'You have to let him go. He isn't worth it.'

'How can you say that?' Karim didn't turn, but his grip relaxed slightly. 'He tried to kill you!'

'But he didn't succeed. And it's over now. It's over. He'll go to jail.'

Karim gave a snarl of contempt, released William and nodded to two of the bodyguards, who immediately responded and took William into custody. 'Yes, he'll go to jail. He has committed a crime in Zangrar, and he will receive his punishment here so that I can personally see that it is just. Get him out of my sight.'

The bodyguards dragged William from the room and Alexa immediately turned back to the injured man. 'Karim, you must call the paramedics.' She dropped onto her knees, swiftly removed the man's jacket, identified where the bleeding was coming from and pressed down on it with the folded jacket. 'I'm so sorry. I'm so sorry I couldn't help you before, but you're going to be fine,' she said soothingly. 'We're going to fly you straight to the hospital.'

Karim barked orders into his telephone, and moments later several paramedics arrived and the man was taken away.

Alexa stood up and wiped her hands on her shirt. Seeing the look of tension and anger on his handsome features, she felt a flash of guilt. 'Thank you. You saved me yet again. It's becoming a habit.' Her hesitant smile faltered under his intimidating glare. 'You're very angry, aren't you?'

'I am so angry with you I could strangle you myself!' His tone was thickened with fury. 'What were you *thinking?* What *possessed* you to fly out to the desert alone?' Ranting and growling like a furious beast, Karim paced the length of the control room and back again. 'You could have been killed. You *would* have been killed if I hadn't arrived when I did.'

Alexa stared at him, stunned that he felt so strongly. 'Yes, that's probably true. I—I was a bit impulsive, but when I heard that there was an explosion and that you wouldn't be able to get here for a while I wanted to come and help.'

He jabbed his fingers through his sleek, dark hair. 'And that was foolish.'

'You wanted a wife who was going to care for the people of Zangrar,' she pointed out softly. 'I care, Karim. Over the past month or so they've welcomed me and made me feel more at home than I've ever felt in my life before. Although it's only been a short time, this feels like my home.'

'You showed the most amazing courage and self sacrifice, as

usual, and I blame myself for the fact that you put yourself at risk today.'

Alexa looked at him in surprise. 'How can you possibly blame yourself?'

'I blame myself on two counts. Firstly, because I am the one who insisted that you show trust and, secondly, because I didn't reveal to you that there was still a risk.'

'You didn't know that he was still going to try and have me killed.'

Karim ran a hand over the back of his neck, unusually hesitant. 'I have had agents working in Zangrar since that night in the cave when you told me your story,' he muttered finally. 'I was aware that he was planning something, but I believed you to be safe because you were within the Citadel. When I learned from Omar that you had flown out to the desert, I almost lost my mind.'

'You guessed that my uncle was behind the explosion?'

'I thought it possible. My agents had started to uncover the beginnings of a conspiracy, but they had no details.'

'But he couldn't have known that I would come myself.'

'It was a reasonable assumption because that's the sort of woman you are. You are strong and compassionate and you care deeply.' Karim reached out and pulled her against him, stroking her hair away from her face. 'It's the reason the people of Rovina love you, the reason that the people of Zangrar love you, and—' He broke off and inhaled deeply. 'And it's the reason that I love you.'

Her heart stumbled. 'You love me?'

'Very much.'

'Y-you never said.'

'I didn't acknowledge it myself until a few hours ago.' Karim stroked her cheek with his fingers. 'When I was told that you had flown out here I suddenly guessed what the conspiracy was, and I knew you were in serious danger. I tried to contact you, but you were already helping the wounded. So I could do nothing except wait, and I thought I was going to go out of my mind. Every minute of the flight through the desert was torture. I had to endure a vivid mental picture of what might have happened to you.'

Alexa placed her hand on his chest, checking that he was real. 'You don't do love.'

'Apparently I do,' Karim drawled softly, lowering his mouth to hers and kissing her gently. 'And it seems that I do it intensely and completely. I love you, *habibati*. You are mine and mine alone, although occasionally I may be prepared to share you with our people.'

His kiss made her dizzy, and when he finally lifted his head it took her a moment to speak. 'I forced you to marry me.'

'And I came to Rovina in person, determined to make you change your mind about marrying the Sultan. But the moment you removed your mask after the fencing match I knew I was in trouble.'

'I was hoping you'd lose so that I could justify firing you. I thought I'd be safer on my own. I didn't trust anyone. I didn't dare.'

'You were feisty and brave and seemed to live up to your title of "rebel princess".'

'I *did* try to tell you that I was in danger.'

'Believe me, I deeply regret the fact that I did not believe you, but you have to understand that all the women in my life up to this point have used drama and hysterics as a means of obtaining what they want.'

'I was being honest.'

Karim gave a driven sigh. 'I know that now. When I discovered everything that you had been through, I just wanted to keep you safe from everyone. That night in the desert—'

'It was so hard for me not to sleep with you,' Alexa admitted softly, faint colour touching her cheeks. 'I wanted you *so* badly.'

'And I wanted you. That was the moment when I decided that the marriage would take place.' He studied her face. 'Perhaps I was already in love with you. I know that you made me feel more alive than I'd felt in years. For a short time, when we were to-gether, I forgot about duty and responsibility.'

'I just wish you'd told me who you were. I was *so* confused. I thought I was marrying the Sultan while in love with another man. It was *horrible*.'

Karim gave a self-satisfied smile. 'Fortunately I am *not* so possessive as to be jealous of myself.'

She placed her hand on his chest and looked up at him. 'You really love me? You're sure?'

He bent his head and kissed her gently. 'My desert princess. I was expecting you to hate everything about my country, and you astonished me. Everything fascinated you. You fell in love with Zangrar, and I—' he murmured the words against her mouth '—I fell in love with you, *habibati*.'

His words brought her emotions rushing to the surface, and Alexa leaned her forehead against his chest to hide her tears. 'Sorry. I'm being stupid. It's just that I'm happy. It's like a dream.'

'But a *good* dream, I hope. Stop crying.' His voice rough, Karim lifted her chin and frowned down at her. 'I forbid you to cry. From now on if anything causes you a moment of unhappi-ness you have only to tell me and it will be dealt with.'

She gave a shaky smile, still dizzy with the novelty of having someone who cared for her. 'What happens now? My uncle—'

'Will stand trial and will undoubtedly spend the rest of his life behind bars.' Karim gave a faint smile. 'Which leaves you with a problem, *habibati*. The Council are now ruling Rovina, but they are eager to welcome their Queen. I presume you don't wish to abdicate this responsibility?'

'No.' Alexa shook her head firmly. 'I owe it to my father to at least try to sort out the mess that William has made. There are so many problems.'

'And so many solutions,' Karim murmured, lowering his head to claim another kiss. 'I am particularly skilled at sorting out the messes left by previous rulers. I can advise you on many shortcuts.'

The touch of his mouth was making it impossible to think. 'You're suggesting we divide our time between Zangrar and Rovina? Can that happen?'

'We will make it happen. Where there is a will and a fleet of private jets…' His casual shrug dismissed the problem to nothing. 'The distance is nothing, and there is much to be said for spending time in both countries. Our children will grow to love the desert, but they will also experience the forests and fields of Rovina. They will have a privileged childhood, experiencing two different cultures, and they will learn to be tolerant. When he is old enough, our first son will rule Zangrar and our second son will rule Rovina.'

Alexa wound her arms around his neck. 'And if we have a daughter?'

'If she is as brave and resourceful as her mother, then she will be able to rule both countries with her eyes shut, while taking her fencing lessons,' Karim drawled, amusement in his dark eyes as he bent his head and kissed her. 'Whatever we decide, our two countries will now be united for ever, and you will be able to implement those changes that your father would have wanted. You have already had some practice spending my money. Feel free to perfect your talents in that direction.'

Touched by his support, Alexa hugged him. 'You make me *so* happy, and no one has ever done that before.'

'Then get used to it, *habibati,*' he purred in a lazy, masculine voice. 'Because I have discovered that I am incredibly committed when it comes to the issue of my wife's happiness. I am willing to knock down anyone who stands in your way.'

'You already did that.' She glanced around the room, taking in the debris and the broken door, still unable to believe the passion and determination with which he'd defended her. 'You saved me. Again.'

'And I intend to carry on saving you, should it be necessary, but it would be nice if you could give me less cause for concern or my hair will be grey before our children have even been born.'

Alexa touched her fingers to his hair, feeling the silken strands and admiring the deep, bold black. 'You don't seem like a man who worries easily.'

'I'm a man who knows how to defend his own.' He hauled her against him in a possessive gesture. 'Remember that, Alexandra.'

'I'll remember it. And, in return, what do you want from me?'

'You know.' Karim's gaze was arrogant and assured. 'I want everything, Alexa. Everything that you have to give, everything that you are. No holding back.'

Loved and secure for the first time in her life, Alexa smiled. 'Is that all, Your Excellency? Well, I don't think that is going to be too hard…'

HIRED: FOR THE BOSS'S PLEASURE

She's gone from personal assistant
to mistress—but now he's demanding
she become the boss's bride!

Read all our fabulous stories this month:

MISTRESS: HIRED FOR THE BILLIONAIRE'S PLEASURE
by INDIA GREY

THE BILLIONAIRE BOSS'S INNOCENT BRIDE
by LINDSAY ARMSTRONG

HER RUTHLESS ITALIAN BOSS
by CHRISTINA HOLLIS

MEDITERRANEAN BOSS, CONVENIENT MISTRESS
by KATHRYN ROSS

Demure but defiant...
Can three international playboys
tame their disobedient brides?

Lynne Graham

presents

Proud, masculine and passionate, these men are used
to having it all. In stories filled with drama, desire
and secrets of the past, find out how these arrogant
husbands capture their hearts.

THE GREEK TYCOON'S
DISOBEDIENT BRIDE
Available December 2008, Book #2779

THE RUTHLESS MAGNATE'S
VIRGIN MISTRESS
Available January 2009, Book #2787

THE SPANISH BILLIONAIRE'S
PREGNANT WIFE
Available February 2009, Book #2795

HARLEQUIN *Presents*

International Billionaires

Life is a game of power and pleasure.
And these men play to win!

Let Harlequin Presents® take you on a jet-set journey
to meet eight male wonders of the world. From rich
tycoons to royal playboys— they're red-hot and ruthless!

International Billionaires coming in 2009

THE PRINCE'S WAITRESS WIFE
by *Sarah Morgan*, February

AT THE ARGENTINEAN BILLIONAIRE'S BIDDING
by *India Grey*, March

THE FRENCH TYCOON'S PREGNANT MISTRESS
by *Abby Green*, April

THE RUTHLESS BILLIONAIRE'S VIRGIN
by *Susan Stephens*, May

THE ITALIAN COUNT'S DEFIANT BRIDE
by *Catherine George*, June

THE SHEIKH'S LOVE-CHILD
by *Kate Hewitt*, July

BLACKMAILED INTO THE GREEK TYCOON'S BED
by *Carol Marinelli*, August

THE VIRGIN SECRETARY'S IMPOSSIBLE BOSS
by *Carol Mortimer*, September

8 volumes in all to collect!

HARLEQUIN *Presents*

kept for his
Pleasure

She's his mistress on demand!

Wherever seduction takes place, these fabulously
wealthy, charismatic, sexy men know how to
keep a woman coming back for more!

She's his mistress on demand—but when he
wants her body *and soul* he will be demanding
a whole lot more! Dare we say it…even marriage!

CONFESSIONS OF A
MILLIONAIRE'S MISTRESS
by **Robyn Grady**

**Don't miss any books in
this exciting new miniseries
from Harlequin Presents!**

HP12801

REQUEST YOUR FREE BOOKS!

2 FREE NOVELS PLUS 2 FREE GIFTS!

You're invited to join our Tell Harlequin Reader Panel!

By joining our new reader panel you will:

- Receive Harlequin® books—they are FREE and yours to keep with no obligation to purchase anything!
- Participate in fun online surveys
- Exchange opinions and ideas with women just like you
- Have a say in our new book ideas and help us publish the best in women's fiction

In addition, you will have a chance to win great prizes and receive special gifts!
See Web site for details. Some conditions apply.
Space is limited.

To join, visit us at
www.TellHarlequin.com.